SHAMEFUL
DUTIES

Sarah Saraband

Shameful Duties

Past Venus Press
London 2007

Past Venus Press

is an imprint of

Erotic Review Books
ERS, 1st Floor, 17 Harwood Road,
LONDON SW6 4QP
Tel: +44 (0) 207 736 5800
Email: enquiries@eroticprints.org
Web: www.eroticprints.org

© 2007 MacHo Ltd, London UK

Illustrations © Mazzza

ISBN : 978-1-904989-38 -7

Printed and bound in Spain by Litografia Rosés. Barcelona

SHAMEFUL DUTIES

Sarah Saraband

SHAMEFUL DUTIES

Sarah Saraband

PROLOGUE

By and large, most Fairview families and individuals led a normal existence. Their dreams and aspirations were no different to the vast majority of middle class America. They woke up to have breakfast before going to earn their daily bread and they returned home after work, pleasantly tired, for the evening meal. The housewives took the children to school, did the marketing and kept the home clean and tidy. At weekends they enjoyed the local amenities, the various social and sporting clubs, they visited friends and relations, they get together for a family meal.

And by and large, most males were content with their lot, the slow climb up the corporate ladder, the promotion and the rewards that come from hard work and a devotion to the job, while most females were happy to date, get engaged, marry, have children and settle down to a life of quiet and contented domesticity,

But then there were some citizens of Fairview who had never known what it was to toil for a company or corporation. That was because they owned one. Or because they were married to someone who did.

It was, indeed, an enviable position to occupy.

Such a man was Victor Jordan, the son of a stationery tycoon and the richest of Fairview's citizens. When his father died, Victor had inherited a business that pretty much ran itself. His life was simple – really there wasn't much to do, work-wise. Of course he had to crack the whip now and again, and sometimes he did. He invested some of the profits in real estate, including the tall apartment block where he had his own, luxury triplex penthouse.

Tall, handsome and fair-haired with a boyish charm that concealed an aggressive and ruthless ambition, Victor could have anything he wanted, or so he thought, until he met young Jessica Douglas, an 18-year-old Amerasian beauty whose mother was Chinese and whose father, now deceased, had been a son of Fairview. Jessie's widowed mother, Mary, was the daughter of poor Chinese immigrants, while Jessie's father had been 'old money' from one of Fairview's more established families.

Artie Douglas had lost most of his considerable fortune by taking part in or backing harebrained schemes that always seemed to lose his stake. Finally he drank himself to death. Jessie's mother had had to sell the old family home, which was no longer in a fashionable part of town, so it fetched little in a sluggish real estate market.

And now Mary and Jessica lived in genteel

poverty not more than a few blocks away from Victor's luxurious dwelling. The young, dark-haired beauty and the good-looking tycoon bumped into each other one day in a local diner and, for Victor, it was lust at first sight. Well, maybe a little more than that, because when he realised that he would not find such a bright, beautiful, spirited and intelligent girl so easily the next time he looked, he thought that he should probably marry her. Because Jessica Douglas's beauty *was* exceptional. With huge, slightly almond-shaped eyes, a cute nose and big, sensuous lips that just begged to be kissed, a slender body with generous, shapely breasts, a deliciously rounded derrière and legs that seemed to go on forever, she would be a wife to make other men instantly jealous. A trophy wife. And Victor liked trophies, and he liked the idea of making others jealous. He liked it very much. And they would be envious for a long time to come, if Jessie's mom was anything to go by.

Mary Douglas was a stunningly attractive woman. With high cheekbones and more typically oriental eyes, though without her daughter's willowy tallness, she had a sexy, curvaceous body that belied her 38 years, and it was easy to guess from whom Jess had acquired those luscious lips and larger-than-average breasts.

But, and it was a big 'but' as far as Victor was concerned, young Jess would have to lose some of those old-fashioned, straight-laced ideas about sex that she seemed to entertain. Jessie was still a virgin, and that was good, as far as the handsome young tycoon was concerned. The fact that he was to be the first to possess and deflower this beauty appealed very much to him. But she was also sexually naive, and although she seemed passionate enough, and was not slow to become aroused, her lack of experience seemed to make her reluctant to experiment with some of the less conventional areas of sex or appreciate the fact that there was more to sex than the missionary position.

The first time that he persuaded her to let him fuck her was just after he had proposed. Jess was besotted by her rich, handsome fiancé and trusted him: the experience was near perfect for both of them; after he had held her in his arms and they had sworn their undying love for each other. But the next evening, when he had suggested that she kneel in front of him, unzip his pants, take his cock out and place it in her mouth and suck it until he ejaculated therein, she not only demurred, but told Victor in no uncertain terms what she would be prepared to do and what she would not in their marital bed – and for that matter – outside it. Victor didn't much care for her list of 'would nots' and, in turn, gave his fiancée his own list of what he thought should be included on the matrimonial menu. Jessie was appalled and, her beautiful eyes blazing, told him that he was 'disgusting'.

This had led to a furious row, and in a trice the engagement was broken.

Jess stormed out of his apartment vowing never to return. Between sobs and sniffles, she recounted the whole sorry tale to her sympathetic, understanding mother. But while Mary was comforting towards her unhappy daughter, but there was also a glint of steel in her eye. When Jessica had announced her engagement, she was thrilled: it would be their salvation, their ticket to a life of comfort, luxury and ease. Their meal ticket. The lovely Chinese woman was not about to lose that dream so easily.

Chapter 1

Mary looked at the kitchen wall clock as she heard the door of Jessie's beat-up old car slam. She was home a little earlier than usual...

Mary stared into the half finished salad as she put down her paring knife. She dreaded the coming session with her daughter, but there was no way to avoid it.

"Hi, Mom – what's for dinner?"

The cheery greeting made Mary smile as she turned to see her pretty dark-haired daughter.

"Jessica, you're as bad as a man. The first thing you're interested in when you get home from work is food."

The girl grinned, her wide, sensuous mouth drawing back to reveal perfect white teeth.

"I guess you're right. That's what Daddy always used to ask about first, wasn't it? Well, I don't blame him – what are we having?"

Mary pretended to be angry.

"Hopeless. You're absolutely hopeless. I don't blame Victor for being fed up with you. I can say one thing for your father – he was interested in food, but there was another subject that he was even more serious about..."

The mention of her former fiancé's name

made Jessie suddenly serious.

"Oh, Mom – let's don't even talk about Victor now. The more I think about it all the more I see that it wouldn't work. I guess I should feel lucky that I found out about his tastes before we got married. It would be terrible to have found it all out afterwards..."

Mary was annoyed with herself; she had not intended to bring up that subject until after dinner. But suddenly she decided to go ahead with it.

"Jessie... honey, sit down for a minute while I finish fixing this salad. I want to talk to you about something... about Victor. Maybe things are not quite as bleak as they seem."

The young girl looked at her mother closely, puzzled by her words.

"Oh, Mom – you just don't know. You weren't there. I haven't even told you everything he said – all the things he wanted to do. It was just awful. It still makes me shiver to think about the things he likes."

"Jessie – sit down. There are some things we have to discuss. I had intended to do it later, but we may as well do it now."

The young Amerasian made no further comment as she put her purse on the table and slipped gracefully into a chair across the table from her still beautiful oriental mother. Mary had been standing as she prepared the salad and she too sank into a chair. For a moment mother and daughter looked at each other without speaking.

Mary took a deep breath and plunged in to a task that she did not relish.

"Jessica, I talked to Victor last night. I went to his apartment, in fact..."

"Mother! How *could* you? How could you do such a thing? I don't want you to go to him begging him to take a girl that he's obviously not satisfied with..."

"Oh, cut it out, Jessica."

Mary's beautiful face wore an unaccustomed frown.

"It wasn't like that at all. Wait until you hear the whole story. You're going to be damn glad I went before this is all over. Or do you want to peck at a typewriter all day long in that silly real estate office until some boy with no more money than you have marries you and gives you four or five babies in a row? Now hear me out, and try to look at all this from a more pragmatic point of view for a change."

* * *

Almost an hour later Jess was still dazed as she stood up and moved uncertainly toward the coffee maker on the stove.

"Mom, I... I just can't believe it. Any of it. That you want to give your body to him, or that he would want both of us under those circumstances, or that you would expect me to go for a plan like that. Us living in Victor's penthouse and having him take both of us. It... it's just so... perverted."

Mary shook her head wearily.

"Give me another cup of coffee, too. You're so stubborn you've given me a headache. Jessie – it's not perverted, it's practical. You've got to see that."

"Practical? That's a funny word for it."

Jess poured both cups and slumped back down in her chair.

"Mom, what you're telling me is that I should marry Victor, and let him fuck me while he uses you for all the other kinds of sex that he likes. On nights when he didn't fuck me you'd suck his prick or let him fuck you in the ass or anything else he wanted."

Her pretty face took on an uncharacteristically sour look.

"I'm using your words now; my vocabulary doesn't seem to be complete enough to cover the situation..."

"Jessica – do you love Victor? If you do, you should see this as a way to avoid losing him. I admit it's a little unconventional, but the point is that you're in love with an unconventional man. And, believe me – it won't be long until your point of view changes and you see things the same way he does. That will happen, I promise you it will. And when it does you'll thank me for the rest of your life for not letting the whole thing blow up in your face now. All this is if you love him, I mean... if you don't, then I don't want any part of it, either. Damn it, do you love him or not?"

Jess was suddenly very quiet as she stared at her mother. When she finally spoke her voice was so low that it was almost unintelligible.

"Yes, Mom. That's just the trouble, I really *do* love him..."

* * *

The drive had been a silent one. Mary did not force a conversation; she realized that, despite a firm decision, her daughter was still torn with doubt as her crucial moment approached. The plan did ask a lot of the pretty young girl, who suddenly broke the silence with a torrent of words.

"Gee, it feels funny to be coming to Victor's apartment like this. I've been there once, and he made love to me, and you've been there once, and he... did the same to you. And tonight he wants to do it to us both – in front of each other. It's weird. You can say what you want to, but it's unnatural. I know it is."

Mary restrained her impatience as she pulled into a parking slot. She tried to remember whether the Lincoln next to her was the same one she had parked by before. Then she turned her attention back to the increasingly nervous girl at her side.

"Oh, Jessica, relax, please. Relax and enjoy what we're going to do. After all, baby, sex is about the nicest thing there is, and you can take my word that Victor is far above average. I suppose in a way that's what's caused the problem. Well, better a man a little oversexed than one undersexed. So just relax and enjoy it when he gets his big… thing inside you. Believe me, that's a feeling that you should savour, not dread…"

Jess opened her mouth and then decided that the chances of making her mother understand were negligible. And, though it was hard to admit even to herself, she was thinking about the exquisite sensations that she would again experience. If only it were not under these circumstances…

The pretty young half-oriental girl sighed as she got out of the car and closed the door.

* * *

"Jessie, I have to admit I'm a little surprised. Pleasantly surprised. Somehow I didn't think you'd go along with your mother's plan."

Victor was smiling in a vulpine way as he brought the seated women their drinks.

"Martinis again, if that's okay with you two. Seems like I've been on a martini kick for a month."

The young girl was silent as she accepted her glass. Mary spoke as she took hers.

"This suits us, Victor. I like martinis and Jessie drinks very little anyway."

"I may get drunk tonight. I may have to drink the entire pitcher." The young girl's voice was petulant.

Victor looked at her narrowly. Her attitude was not what he had hoped for; obviously her acceptance of the situation was grudging. She would have to be shown the error of her ways. The sooner she was made to understand her exact place in the scheme of things the better for all concerned.

His voice was friendly, and at first both women missed the veiled threat in it.

"Jessie, baby, you don't seem too happy about it all. Now, I want to be sure – do you or do you not want to take part in your mother's plan? Answer carefully."

Jess's voice sounded slightly sulky.

"I'm here, aren't I? I don't pretend to like everything about the situation..."

"The crucial point is whether you accept it, not whether you like it. You'll come to like it, in time... Now – the point at the moment is that I'm not entirely satisfied with your attitude and I intend to change it. As a first step in that direction I want you to understand more clearly your place in all this. Stand up, Jess. I want you to raise your skirt, slip your panties off, and show me your cunt."

Victor's unexpected demand shocked both women. Jessie stared stupidly at him, too numbed to reply. Even Mary did not react with typical promptness; her first thought was that

Victor was not handling Jessie in the right way.

"Jessica – I told you to do something. Is it possible that you failed to hear me?"

The startled girl finally found her tongue.

"Victor! What's wrong with you? How can you say such things – and in front of Mother?"

The man closed his eyes as if in weary disgust for a moment, then took a long sip of his drink before he replied. When he spoke there was an exasperation in his voice.

"Alright, Jess. I'll go through this one time, and no more. If you want to marry me you'll have to accept me as I am, because I have no intention of changing, at least any further than the concessions that I've already made. You know what those concessions are – I've agreed that I'll expect only straight fucking from you; the refinements I'll get from Mary. But I do expect to be obeyed without question when I tell you to do something. What I want now involves only a look at your cunt; it certainly does not violate our agreement. Jess, you have to decide, once and for all. Either you'll do what I want, without questions or delay, or we'll have to forget the whole thing. Am I loud and clear?"

Mary held her breath; she was not sure that Victor's severe attitude would work. Jess had a quietly rebellious streak and had never been completely sold on the whole plan...

Jessie stared into her lover's eyes as her mind struggled to evaluate the alternatives. He was clearly asking for a sexual situation that she found revolting, but somehow this did not seem to alter her basic need for this strange man... And obviously he would tolerate no further half measures and indecision.

She really had no choice; her mental threshings were beside the point. Jessie lowered her eyes when she spoke.

"Alright, Victor... whatever you say. I just hope you won't take advantage of me. I never thought I'd give in to a man like this..."

Victor Jordan recognized the pretty young girl's final capitulation. But he showed neither surprise nor pleasure.

"Alright then, Jess. You know what I want you to do."

Jessie made no reply as she looked at him for a moment, then put her drink down and slowly got to her feet. Dressed in a clinging silk dress, she faced him, then moved slightly away from the couch and turned again to him.

"Is... this alright? Can you see what you want to from there?"

Victor sounded impatient.

"See *what*, Jessie? Dammit, among other things you've got to learn to use the language. What is it that I want to see?"

Jessie was surprised by her own lack of hesitation.

"My cunt, Victor. You want to see my cunt. There – is that the way you want me to talk? Alright, I'll do it. I'll show you my... cunt"

The svelte young brunette suited action to her words; she slowly pulled the hem of her skirt up to her slim waist, leaving her loins protected only by sheer panties. But that protection was brief; after a moment she hooked her thumbs in their waistband and started them on a slow journey down her impossibly long, tapering legs. Finally they were just a little puddle of material on the floor at her feet.

Jessie stepped out of them gracefully, then bent over to pick them up. When she straightened she instinctively brought the panties in front of her triangle of curly black pubic hair.

But even before Victor could speak the young girl anticipated his reaction to her automatic modesty. She flung the panties to the coffee table in front of the couch and turned to face the man directly.

Victor smiled faintly as his eyes roved over the dark curls and the pink vaginal lips that those curls only partially concealed. He remembered Mary's pubic hair; the two beautiful females were as alike as could be expected for mother and daughter – and the result of a mixed-race marriage. Finally he looked up into Jessie's dark and slightly almond-shaped eyes.

"Nice, Jess – very nice. At least as far as I can see. I really can't tell much about your pussy. Come a little closer and spread your legs and then open your cunt with your fingers. I've fucked it, but I haven't really seen it..."

Jess felt her body respond to the peculiar

sensuality of the scene that Victor was creating. The things he asked were still vaguely repugnant to her nature, but those feelings were fading into the background to make way for more erotic reactions. And those reactions were present; Jess felt a familiar throb in her vagina and she sensed that her nipples were becoming hard and sensitive in the confinement of her bra cups. Damn – he hadn't even touched her...

"Come on, Jessie. Spread your legs and open the lips a little. Your cunt looks good enough to eat – an act which, by the way, you can expect to see me perform on your mother's cunt. I have a feeling it won't be long before you realize what you're missing. That's it – good. Move your legs just a little further apart. Fine. That makes your cunt lips separate a little bit. But not enough – take your fingers and pull them a little wider, then after I have a good look I want you to put a finger up your cunt as far as you can. What about that, darling – do you like to finger fuck yourself?"

The question brought back a wave of embarrassment and caused Jessie's face to flush. It had hit home. The twenty-year-old had indeed used her fingers in the past as a means of solitary pleasure.

She did not answer as she brought both hands between her spread thighs and held her vaginal lips apart with the fingers of one while the forefinger of the other hand gently invaded the little crevice of her femininity. Jessie felt mortified; this was beyond question the most lewd, brazen thing she had ever done. And yet it was also certain that her libido was responding wildly; her vagina was becoming increasingly wet and sensitive and she knew that a caress of little clitoris would send her over the brink of orgasm almost instantly. And also she sensed that the intensity of her reaction was more because she was masturbating herself in front of Victor and her mother than from the act itself.

And Jessie was not the only person to be aroused at the sight of her fingers busy in her own vagina. Without taking his eyes off the superbly feminine sight in front of him Victor spoke to the older woman seated beside him.

"Mary – honey, this daughter of yours has got my prick hard. Come here and get it out and see what you can do for it. But go easy – I don't want to come this way..."

Mary was entirely willing to comply with the man's request. She had also been affected by her daughter's enforced lewdness, and to a greater extent than she had thought possible. She was glad to have a male object to focus her attention on.

Mary moved closer to Victor as her eyes went to the pronounced bulge in the crotch of his trousers. You're big already, she thought. The sight of Jessie's cunt was all it took...

Victor now had more than visual stimulation. Mary's soft hand closed around his penis under his trousers and began to squeeze and pull the hard organ.

"Damn, Mary – get it out. Don't jack me off in my pants. Get my prick out and play with it."

Mary was happy enough to perform that service. She drew her hand slowly out of his clothes, bringing with it the firm shaft of his penis. Her delicate white hand automatically pumped slowly as her eyes feasted on the male sight.

And Jessie's eyes were large and bright as they, too, focused on her fiancé's large penis even as her fingers continued to work their magic on her own vagina.

"Oh, Victor, I... I never thought..." Jessie's words ended in a self-conscious blush.

Victor's attention went again to the young girl masturbating slowly and sensuously in front of him.

"You never what, honey? Never had a good look at a man's prick before? That's the trouble with quick fucks in the back seat of a car – the kind of fucks that 'nice' girls give their dates. You can never do the job properly like that. And if there's anything that justifies being done right, it's fucking."

As he spoke Jessie continued to finger her vagina in front of him while Mary slowly pumped his penis in her clasping hand. She felt the familiar wetness in her own vagina and almost envied her daughter's opportunity for relief.

Then Mary felt Victor's hand cover hers and halt her manipulation of his penis. She looked at him in surprise, but his words brought quick understanding.

"Hold up, Mary. You're making me come along too fast. Tell you what, let's all go in the bedroom and undress. This time I want to see your body. The other time we never did undress when you sucked my prick."

He paused and turned to Jess, who had stopped the movement of her fingers in her vagina, but had not removed them.

"You, too, honey. I want to see you. I had you undressed when I fucked you, but in deference to your maidenly modesty I left all the lights off. This time I want a good look at both of you, and I want you to get a good look at me and at each other."

Victor paused again and turned back to Mary, who still had her hand clasped around his erection.

"Of course you did get a good look at my prick, I guess, when you sucked it. Well, you'll get a chance to see it again. But not while you suck it; I think we'll do something different this time. Come on – let's go to the bedroom."

Mary finally released him as they stood up. Jessie almost reluctantly let her finger slip from her vagina and let her skirt drop, but she made no move to recover her panties from the coffee table where she had thrown them. Her emotions were mixed; she dreaded the coming encounter in a way, but she was also aware of a growing need for relief for her aroused body.

The trip to the bedroom was brief and slightly ludicrous in its appearance: Victor took the arms of the two seemingly fully-dressed females and guided them to his bedroom with his erect penis waving cheerfully in front of him. Once in the bedroom he began to undress quickly. The room reeked of masculine achievement. A dark, plum-coloured wallpaper complemented rich mahogany fitted cupboards, as well as tables and chairs in polished teak. Various shiny brass artefacts were dotted around the room: a big ship's compass, a telescope, a sextant; the lantern-like wall brackets were also of burnished, gleaming brass. As well as silver sporting trophies, large lumps of exotic or semi-precious stones, such as amethyst, agate or malachite, lay haphazardly around, while old English coaching prints hung on the walls. In the centre of one of the large room's walls, between two bedside tables with lamps, was an emperor-sized bed, the very epicentre of Victor's bachelor lair.

But there was no time for a guided tour.

"Okay girls – strip. And let's make it quick this time. There'll be times in the future when I'll want to see a slow, teasing job of it, but not now. I'm already worked up; I just want to get my prick up a cunt."

Jessie was less nervous than she had expected to be, but she was still embarrassed by the prospect of undressing in the brightly-lit room before her lover and mother. But her hesitation was more than offset by her very real physical needs, and she began to remove her dress without undue delay. She was glad that her panties had already been removed; she knew that they would have been soaked by now by the juices of her arousal.

Mary also undressed quickly. She, too, was aroused, and she was anxious for the man to get the full impact of her lush body. Their previous encounter had been an odd-ball one; she could not recall a previous instance in which she had given a man complete satisfaction while fully dressed... Mary's blouse, her pencil skirt and then her panties and bra were quickly stripped off of her lovely body and thrown carelessly on the thick carpet.

And then all three people were nude. Victor's eyes went from mother to daughter and then back again as they feasted on the exquisite femininity at his disposal. The two women were both voluptuous and lovely; Jessie was what Mary must have been a decade and a half ago. And Jessie would be extremely lucky if she resembled her mother fifteen years from now. The thought flitted through Victor's mind that it was possible that he would still have these two females at that time.

Then his immediate physical needs snapped his mind back to the present. His penis was so hard that it almost hurt.

"Well, I have to admit that you two are quite a pair. Mary, your plan looks better than ever, assuming that Jessie is properly cooperative, of course."

He paused and grinned as he looked at the pretty young girl's lust filled face.

"And I have an idea she will be, because I think she needs a good fucking as bad as I do. That right, honey?"

Jessie blushed a shade deeper, but she looked at Victor squarely.

"I… I am worked up, honey. I… yes, I want to be… fucked. Please fuck me… I want your prick up my… pussy. Please…?"

Jessie's frank words caught Victor by surprise and made his penis twitch. He had expected to have to force her to use such language, but apparently the pretty girl was so aroused that she used it instinctively.

"Jessie… don't worry, you're gonna get fucked. Right now. I was going to… hell, that can wait. Right now I got to fuck that sweet little pussy of yours. Come on to bed, sweetheart…"

Victor held out his hand to Jessie and escorted the lovely girl the few short steps to the bed in a fashion that would have seemed ludicrous to a disinterested spectator. But it was likely that such a thing as a disinterested spectator was a distinct impossibility; certainly Mary was far from disinterested as she watched the man take her naked daughter to the bed. Entirely out of the action for the moment, Mary moved closer to the bed so that she could see the coming events. She was not even aware that she was standing in a rather ungraceful position with her legs slightly apart and one forefinger already between her seeping labia.

On the bed Victor had forsaken his usual foreplay for direct action. He put the willing girl on her back and moved beside her as he ran one hand in between her soft thighs.

"Okay, Jessie, spread your legs. I'm gonna leave out all the extras this time. I'm gonna fuck hell outa that pretty little cunt. How does that sound to you?"

Jessie's hand stole down to his loins in a quickly successful search for his penis as she answered.

"Oh, Victor, I'm ready. My... cunt's ready for your prick. Fuck me, darling, I can't wait. Please... Hurry, fuck me. I want your prick inside me."

Again surprised by Jessie's lewd language, Victor stopped feeling between her legs. Her vagina was soft and ready, and his penis was hard and ready...

He gave a little grunt of passion as he rolled between Jessie's spread thighs. She bent her knees as she brought them up above his back while he adjusted his cock so that its head could find the warm and wet groove of her sex. His unguided penis rubbed fitfully in the soft curls of her pubic down.

But he could not resist one refinement. He

started to tell the aroused girl beneath him to take his organ and make the insertion, then he decided to delay long enough to let Mary guide his penis into her daughter's vagina.

He turned his half-closed eyes to the side of the bed. After a moment he made them focus on Mary as she stood there fingering her cunt. Victor grinned fleetingly; he was too aroused himself to make the obvious jokes about Mary's activity.

"Mary, baby – come on over here and help me. Want you to put my prick in her cunt. Come on – it's not every mother that gets to help her daughter fuck."

Mary did not respond immediately as she looked at Victor and tried to interpret his motives. She probably had little choice, short of fouling up the whole situation, but her response would at least be rather different if he was being deliberately degrading in his actions.

But she decided quickly that he was merely adding interesting refinements to his procedure. And Mary had no objection to this; on the contrary, she welcomed the opportunity for a close view of the entry of his penis into Jessie's young body.

The beautiful Oriental's smile was enigmatic as she moved to the bed and stooped over to run a hand in between their bodies. She grasped his penis and, surprised to find that it was even larger that it had been before, couldn't help commenting on the fact.

"Victor – you must be ready. Your prick's harder than ever…"

But Victor was impatient.

"Damn, baby, don't play with it. Go on – stick it in her cunt. You'll jack me off if you keep fooling with my prick."

Mary giggled as she tried to follow his instruction. She brought the almost purple head of the throbbing shaft to Jessie's dark pubic curls and rubbed it on the soft, pink lips of her femininity. But the actual entry was easier said than done, and Mary found it necessary to work her other hand into the cramped space between their bodies so that she could open her daughter's vaginal lips with her fingers. Mary pulled on his penis.

"Alright, Victor, put it in. I can't do it all for you – you have to do some of your fucking yourself…"

The man did not hear her as his hard, thick organ slid into Jessie's inexperienced young body and he slipped into some sort of incipient ecstasy. Mary withdrew her hands quickly as he plunged to full depth in Jessie's excited channel.

"Oh! oh, Victor… you're so deep. Your prick fills my cunt so… oh, just leave it deep in me for a second. It feels so good…"

Jessie's eyes were closed as her lovely straight black hair threshed from side to side while the man supported his torso above her on stiff arms. His eyes were almost shut as he delighted in the feeling that Jessie's tight little vagina produced as it nipped at his hard organ. But he saw the enticing sight that her full, pointed breasts made as they quivered and thrust up towards him and his eyes popped full open again. Jessie's knees and calves twitched at his sides and finally locked across his back...

Mary was now lying on her side on the edge of the bed as she watched the man prepare to begin his strokes of passion into her daughter's willing body. And there was no doubt of Jessie's willingness; she moaned in pleasure as her arms went around Victor's neck and drew him down to her superb, tip-tilted breasts.

"Victor – darling, go on, fuck me. Move your prick in my cunt. Oh, it's so wonderful. Fuck me, darling – I'm going to come."

And that was Victor's problem, the reason that he had not already begun his motion. He knew that his orgasm was near and that any serious stroking would trigger it. He was reluctant to give up the pleasure of impalement in Jessie's young body so quickly, and so he lay on her with his penis at full depth in her vagina while he made only the most subtle rotary motions as he strove to find the narrow path between further stimulation and climax.

But Jess was not to be denied. She began to rock her young hips beneath him as she urged him to begin the motions of love. "Victor, please – fuck me. Stroke my cunt with your prick, darling. Please – I need it. You've got to fuck me – hurry, darling."

And he could not resist her pleas or his own desires. With a little curse of desperation, Victor pulled his throbbing organ almost out of Jessie's little body and immediately plunged it back to the full depth of her vagina in a thrust that was almost vicious.

Jess squealed in delight as her legs threshed uncontrollably. "Oh God, Victor, fuck me, FUCK MEEE! That's soooo gooood, it's just wonderful..."

So close to the copulating pair that she could feel the slap of Victor's balls on her lovely daughter's upturned anus and the slight sloshing sound as his rod drove in and retreated, Mary's own arousal was reaching boiling point as she watched her daughter take the man's penis deep into her young body. The Chinese woman's fingers were back at her own loins as one invaded her vulva while a thumb strummed her sensitive clitoris.

Victor plunged blindly in and out of Jess with a lack of finesse that was unusual for him. He had given up on all the refinements for this session; they would have to come later under more controlled conditions. For the present he could only give way to his basic needs and rut into this young girl's sweet vagina like an inexperienced schoolboy... And he would not have even this crude but wonderful pleasure for long.

Now he felt the beginning surges of his orgasm as his balls contracted and rose high in

their tightened scrotal sac.

"Jess, I'm coming! I'm there! Oh, you sweet damn fuck... take it – take my come! I'm shootin'! Take my come up your pussy..."

His words and the slashing organ in her tender body pushed Jessie over the brink. She closed her eyes and moaned unintelligibly as a thin rill of saliva trickled out of her gasping mouth.

"Go on, darling, I'm with you. I'm coming! I'm coming! I feel your come shoot in me. Oh, fill my cunt full. Fuck me, darling, always fuck me, fuck me..."

And the third person in the room also reached orgasm as the sensual words of the two people in front of her combined with the efforts of her own fingers to bring Mary a culmination that was only slightly less intense than that found by Jessie and Victor. Mary's eyes stayed on the penis pumping into her daughter's body as her own orgasm peaked and then began to subside. She even saw a little gush of whitish semen escape Jessie's vulva and run down the crease between her threshing buttocks. Mary finally closed her eyes and sighed as she tried to stem her own vaginal sensations by bringing her working fingers to a halt in the liquid channel. But she could not close her ears to Jessie's passionate mewling, and Mary began to realize for the first time what a sensual young woman her daughter had become as she listened to her passionate, babbling words.

"... so good. Victor, I never realized... this time I'm sure I felt it when you came. It's as if I sensed your come squirt out of your prick and into my cunt. Maybe I felt it go in my womb – do you think that's possible? I just know when I came it was perfect. Oh, if this is how you want to fuck me, Victor, darling, I want you to fuck me all the time."

The satisfied and exhausted man was a little surprised by Jessie's words as she squirmed gently beneath him. His shrunken penis was still in her vagina, and he could feel the pool of semen which now filled her femininity. "Jess baby, you sound like you're seeing the light. You're right – fucking is good, but it's not the whole story. I'll show you other things that'll really blast you off. You'll see what I mean when I suck your cunt, and you suck my prick..."

His words made Jessie's euphoria evaporate. She had been enthralled by the exquisite sensations of her orgasm, but she was by no means ready to abandon herself to these other perverted acts that he seemed to be so interested in. If he insisted on those he would have to do them with her mother, as the plan had specified.

Her mother... For the first time since the insertion of his penis Jessie thought about Mary. She turned questioning eyes to the side and was both startled and embarrassed to see her naked mother lying on the edge of the bed facing them... Oh god, she had seen the whole thing

– she had seen Victor's prick moving in and out of her cunt, and she had heard the things that they said… What a thing for a girl's mother to see!

Victor raised himself slightly off of Jessie's breasts, now pink and suffused with fulfilled desire, as he looked down into her perspiration-streaked face.

"Jess… honey, you hear what I said? We can start some real loving now that you're seeing things right. I knew you'd come around, baby – I just wasn't sure how soon."

Jessie turned away from her mother and looked up into Victor's face. She realized that he had misunderstood her, that perhaps for a moment she had misunderstood herself. She did enjoy his love making, but those other things were still out of the question.

"Oh, Victor – I didn't mean… I did enjoy you fucking me, I admit it. But those other things… darling, you agreed that I wouldn't have to do them – that mother would take care of that." Her voice took on a pleading quality. "Please, darling, you agreed…"

Victor sighed as he pulled his shrunken penis from Jessie's body and rolled off of her to slump down between the two women. Damn, for a minute he had thought…

"Okay, Jessie, I'll stick to the agreement; it's just that for a minute I thought you'd come out of your damn shell. Beats me how you can enjoy fucking so much and still be so damn prudish about the rest. Well, like I said, you'll come around... umf!"

The man's little exclamation was caused by his surprise at the feeling of a feminine hand again on his penis. Mary's orgasm had been a relatively light one, and her powerful libido was ready for further action. She had intended to pause so that all of them could wash and recuperate, but she suddenly found her hand going instinctively to his male organ. Its condition was not discouraging; it was not completely soft, and it began to twitch and throb in response to her hand's skilful stroking. The shaft was wet and sticky with the combined juices of the copulating couple, but Mary had never been repulsed by male sperm...

She squirmed closer to him and brought one lush breast against his arm as her experienced hand began to work in earnest on his deflated penis. Mary moved her face against his ear and began to nibble on the lobe and then ran her tongue in the little opening.

"Victor – dear, I need a little attention from this sweet prick of yours. He seems all worn out at the moment, but I'll put him back in shape. Honey, if you want some more loving, I'll give it to you. Anything you want. But remember, I want to come, too. What do you want, honey? Want Mary to suck your prick again?"

Victor lay staring at the ceiling as he savoured her expert touch on his hardening penis and considered her offer. Well, since Jessie refused...

he rolled partially toward Mary, careful not to interfere with her busy hand at his loins.

"Okay, sweet, you deserve some fun, too. But I don't want a blow job right now – I'll probably take a long time to come this quick after screwing Jessie. Tell you what – I think I'd like to bugger you. Can you come from being fucked in the ass?"

Mary drew in a sharp breath; she had not quite expected this. But it was part of the agreement, and she had no real objection. The act was one that she had not performed in a long time and it would probably hurt a little until she got used to it again, but she should have no trouble reaching orgasm.

"Why… yes, Victor, I… I usually can. You'll have to go easy with me; I haven't done it in some time."

The man laughed as he felt his penis harden in her fingers.

"You know me, baby – 'easy old Victor'. I'll go slow as you want. Probably couldn't come quick if I wanted to. Feel my prick? The idea of fucking your asshole's gettin' it stiff again."

Mary giggled almost girlishly.

"I've noticed. I don't see how you can get hard this quick. Victor, I believe you need two women to take care of this prick you've got. I've never seen one quite like it."

"Glad you appreciate real talent," he said. " Now, if we can just get this silly daughter of yours to see things the way you do…"

"She will. But right now just concentrate on me. I need it. See what you've done?"

Mary's question referred to the condition of her sex; her free hand had grasped one of his and led it to the centre of her weeping vaginal cleft. He needed no further urging; his experienced fingers slipped into the wet channel and then found the little knob of her enlarged clitoris.

Mary's slim hips jerked in an involuntary spasm as she reacted to his touch. It felt good – very good. Her own hand tightened on his penis and began a stroking action as it reached almost full hardness. While her complimentary comment about his sexual abilities had been mostly for his benefit, the fact remained that he did seem to have a little extra something going for him.

Both participants were ready for more direct action. Mary's mouth was still close to his ear as she lay beside him.

"Honey, I think you're ready, and I know I am. But I think we need something on that lovely cock of yours if you're going to bugger me. It's still slick with your come but that won't last when you put it in my asshole. Have you got some Vaseline?"

Victor immediately saw the wisdom in Mary's remark and a pleasant little extra feature occurred to him. He twisted slightly to look at the young girl who lay, temporarily forgotten, at his other side.

"Jess, your mother's right, we should use a

lubricant. Get that jar out of the drawer in the table on your side of the bed. How would you like to do the honours?"

Jessie did not catch the full implication of his question as she turned and raised up on one elbow to open the table drawer. She rolled back toward the man and held the jar out to him.

"Here you are, Victor."

But he did not take it. He grinned as his hand continued to stroke Mary's sex while her hand pumped slowly on his now erect penis.

"Jessie, baby – I asked how you'd like to do it – put it on for us? You can rub it on my prick and in your mother's asshole. Bet you've never done that before."

Jessie experienced a strange feeling as she understood his lewd request. She felt an initial stab of the expected reaction – shame and embarrassment that he should ask such a vulgar thing. But this response was rather quickly replaced by another one that was more compatible with his plan. What would it be like to do it? She had already secretly begun to enjoy handling his penis, and though the thought of fingering her beautiful mother's anus was not appealing, there was an element of curiosity involved that offset most of her reluctance. And, besides, she had no real choice, short of causing a major argument over a fairly small point...

"Victor, I... oh, you're terrible. You shouldn't ask me to do something like this. With my own mother... for that matter, you shouldn't want to do such a thing yourself. It's just not proper..."

The man chuckled.

"Well, I can agree with a little of that. It's probably not proper. Of course there are people who seem to think that no sex is proper. Fortunately they're losing control of public standards. But, hell – at the moment I'm not worried about public morality. What I want is to fuck your momma's butt, and I want you to help me. Come on, honey, we're ready. Put some of that on my prick, then I'll have your mother get up on her hands and knees so you can get some up her asshole."

Jessie flushed at his words, but she made no protest. She removed the jar's lid, then hooked a dainty finger into the thick lubricant and pulled out a glob which she quickly smoothed onto the head of his penis. For a moment she felt her mother's hand on the thick organ as Mary continued to stroke the base of it while Jessie smeared the head with the greyish goo. But Mary moved her hand away as Jessie began to work down the shaft...

"Okay, that's good. Now for Mary."

Victor turned back to look at the impatient Chinese woman who lay at his side. "What do you think? I believe you might as well just get in position for the fuck. I'm gonna screw your butt doggie fashion, so get on your hands and knees and spread your cheeks. Jessie can work the Vaseline up your asshole. Okay?"

Mary's aroused body was more than ready.

Even the particular act he proposed, never among her favorite sexual variations, now seemed highly attractive.

"Yes, Victor – it's okay with me. Just hurry – you've got me all worked up and I want your prick up me."

The beautiful, mature woman moved gracefully to a position near the centre of the large bed as Victor and Jessie moved slightly to give her the room she needed. She knelt on spread knees, then, with a smile at both of them, leaned forward so that her heavy, swinging breasts brushed the bed as she rested on her elbows and forearms. She wiggled slightly to find the most comfortable position, then turned bright, excited eyes toward her pretty young daughter.

"All right, darling. Put the Vaseline in my bottom-hole. Hurry, baby, mother needs to be fucked... no, I need to be *buggered*."

Aroused rather than repulsed by the vulgarity of her mother's words, Jess moved toward her exposed bottom and looked at the lush buttocks. She had seen those buttocks before, under casual, non-sexual circumstances, but this time they seemed to have an entirely new significance, as did all of her mother's lush body. Mary somehow now seemed to personify sex... lustful, pleasurable sex for sex's sake.

But another spectator grew impatient. Victor's voice disclosed his own renewed passion.

"Go on Jess, hurry. Got to get my prick in her..."

And suddenly Jess herself was anxious to perform her sensual chore. She leaned over Mary's exposed bottom and separated the firm white buttocks with one hand, bringing into view the dark brown, puckered little aperture that was her mother's anus. She stared in fascination at the dainty orfice; it was the first asshole that she had really ever seen up close.

"Jessie, baby – move. Her asshole is pretty, sure, but I got a better use for it than just lookin' at it."

Victor's words prodded the young girl into motion. With almost no remaining reluctance she brought her petroleum jelly smeared fingers up to the crease between Mary's buttocks. She explored the crevice briefly, then brought her fingers to the little anus itself and began to gently force the greasy substance into the tight opening.

Jessie felt her mother's hips quiver as her finger invaded the entrance of the clasping channel. The young girl was surprised by her own stimulation; this act, which would ordinarily seem perverted, now seemed perfectly natural. And interesting, too.

But Jessie's venture into this new sexual area was to be brief. The sight of her attention to her mother's rectum was also a powerful stimulant to the man who was already impatient.

"Jess, move. Get away from her ass, I can't

wait any longer to fuck it. No – wait. Want you to take my prick and stick it in. You can see how to do it better than we can. Hurry – take my prick..."

Jessie's mind was in a daze compounded of sexual arousal and surprise at her part in the activity. But she moved instinctively to carry out his instructions; her hand went once more to his crotch to grasp his now familiar penis while the fingers of her other hand again spread her mother's buttocks to reveal the neat, brown little anus. And then Jessie brought male and female together; as Victor moved awkwardly on his knees to come closer to Mary's waiting bottom Jessie successfully guided the head of his penis to the crinkled little sphincter that was the opening to her mother's rectum.

"There – there, Victor. It'll go in – push it in mother's ass. Oh, damn..."

Jessie's distraught words were spoken mostly to herself as she realized that one of her hands had, seemingly on its own initiative, gone to her own loins and invaded the still soaked channel of her vagina. The fingers automatically sought out her clitoris.

Jessie's eyes were closed as she swayed on her spread knees on the bed. She was only dimly aware of Victor's little shout as he penetrated her mother's bottom, the older woman giving a deep '*ohhhh!*' as she felt the hard penis penetrate her most private place; the evening's unprecedented combination of sex and alcohol had almost overcome the young girl. And when her rubbing, plunging fingers brought on her orgasm the combination proved to be too much. She blacked out as she pitched forward on the bed in an erotic swoon. In a reflex action her fingers continued to work in her little vagina as Victor and Mary began to hunch and buck in their own efforts to find release.

The pain had been there to begin with. Try as she might, Mary had not been able to relax enough to avoid that initial burn as her protesting sphincter reluctantly surrendered to the invader. Then a sort of dull pain as Victor's sizeable cock surged forwards into her rectum. Her mother had once told her that if she was to avoid getting pregnant but have fun and keep her man, she should always try to have sex in this way. She was surprised that her mother even knew about such things, let alone condoned or suggested them. But over the years, she had been grateful for the maternal advice. Before the days of easy contraception, you took it in your mouth or, if you wanted to go further, up your ass. Mary had developed a technique that few men were able to resist. Instead of continuing to relax her anal muscles once they had become accustomed to the unnatural entry, she would actually tighten her asshole on her lover's outstroke, thereby heightening his pleasure tenfold.

As she fingered her clitoris, stimulating the small, protruding organ in long, firm strokes, she attempted once more to practice this trick on

Victor. The results were pleasingly successful. She hadn't lost the knack. After a few 'squeezes', her daughter's fiancé tensed, then cursed, then finally collapsed on top of her, twitching and jerking uncontrollably, more like an epileptic than a suave young lover as he unloaded his tight, sperm-laden balls.

Finally he collapsed sideways and his semi-hard cock pulled out of Mary with and obscene little noise, as if she were breaking wind. Despite the fact she knew such a thing was beyond her control, Mary still blushed as she felt the warm sperm trickle out of her and course down the inside of her thighs. Still on her knees, she used the slippery come as a lubricant, increasing the speed of her self-stimulation until she, too, came in a welter of groans and shuddering sighs.

Chapter 2

"Good morning, Mr. Jordan."

"Good morning."

Victor glanced at the timeclock as he passed his secretary's desk. Nearly ten... damn, he thought, I ought to get here a little earlier... Well, hell – one of the few advantages of owning a business these days was the privilege of setting your own hours.

In his private office, Victor threw his briefcase on the desk and his coat on the couch. He moved to the picture window behind the desk and stared out into the back lot of the family stationery and printing business. A sixth sense, developed partly from his own experience and partly inherited from his father, enabled Victor to feel the status of his business from watching the activity in the lot. His intuition was, in some ways, a more dependable guide than his accountant's financial reports. The feeling that he got today was a satisfactory one – he could see three lorries all bearing the 'JORDAN STATIONERY' logo on their side being loaded – but it did nothing to offset the nagging conviction that had formed in his mind six months ago that he would have to spend more time on his business if he expected further growth. And he'd better keep his eye on that new competitor from the neighbouring state who had recently set up on the south side...

"Victor..."

The feminine voice made him turn. His secretary smiled as she approached him. Her approaches were always an event of interest. At twenty-two years of age, Betty's physical development had peaked, in more ways than one. The two most obvious peaks, and the ones that had prompted Victor to hire her over a year ago, were now only mildly restrained in the cups of a size 38 D brassiere.

The pretty brunette smiled as his eyes made

his routine check of her bosom. Betty wore, as she always did, a cream-coloured blouse, opened to the third button down, that made his inspection both efficient and pleasurable.

"Victor, you never seem to get tired of them. Although I must say that you haven't done much with them lately. Not since you got so tied up with your girlfriend – or is it fiancée?" Betty pouted prettily. "I ought to be jealous."

Victor grinned. He had a genuine affection for his secretary; they understood each other perfectly and served each other's needs well. Her lush body was always available to him, in the office or at her apartment, and he had made considerable use of that availability. In turn her pay was far above average, and she also valued the real friendship that had developed between them. Betty was perhaps the one person from whom Victor had no secrets. But he had neglected her lately...

"I know, baby. But since I started fucking Jessica – and now her mother – I just don't have quite as much left over as I used to. Don't worry – once things have settled down I'm gonna take better care of you. Besides, I doubt that you've been hard up..."

The pretty brunette perched on the corner of his desk in a pose that pulled her tan miniskirt up high enough to show a hint of her panties. She was still smiling, but her tone was serious.

"Well, I won't say I haven't had *any*, but I really don't see anybody much now. They all just seem to want to fuck me and nothing else, and a girl gets tired of that. Well, not tired of fucking, exactly, but even when you're not looking for a love affair you like to at least sense of some sort of friendship. I… well, I guess that's why I give my cunt and everything else to you – I feel like we're friends."

Betty paused and suddenly blushed slightly.

"My God – what a way to be talking at this time of the morning. I was beginning to sound like something out of a woman's confession magazine, wasn't I? Don't mind me…"

Victor put a hand on the soft but firm flesh of her thigh and ran his fingers up into the intimate area between her legs just below her panties. But, strangely, the caress was not a sensual one. For once, his probing fingers managed to express his more tender feelings for the girl over and above a mere appreciation of her body.

Betty seemed embarrassed by this tacit disclosure. She suddenly stood up and let her skirt fall as far as it would as she tried to assume a businesslike air.

"Well, if you're going to be here this morning I have quite a stock of invoices that bookkeeping wants you to initial. And Mrs. O'Connor is here about the company hostess job. Jill Feinberg is due in less than an hour for the same position. Do you want to see Mrs. O'Connor now?"

The mention of the woman's name startled Victor; he had forgotten about the appointments for interview that he had made several days ago.

His reaction was mixed; he was really not in the mood for this sort of thing this morning. Still, an interview of this kind had to be interesting...

He looked up at Betty. "She look okay?"

The girl nodded. "She's pretty. Has a good figure. She should be okay if her attitude's right."

Victor flashed a grin up at his secretary as he fished in a desk drawer for the file folder with the woman's application.

"Yeah, attitude – that's what keeps you from handling this job yourself..."

The expression that crossed the girl's face made him instantly regret his remark. There was a suggestion of hurt feelings and some anger in her voice.

"Damn it, Vic, I don't appreciate that. I tried to make it clear a long time ago that my pussy wasn't always available to your damn customers. If ever I screw your customers it's because I'm doing it as a favour to you - a really *big* favour. I don't ask for any money for that and I don't expect to be paid, either. And in return you treat me like a whore. Maybe I am, in a way, because I work for you and let you fuck me as and when you want. And because, occasionally, I let your customers fuck me, too. But I... oh, hell, if you don't understand by now you never will. I'll send Mrs. O'Connor in."

Her eyes bright with unshed tears, Betty whirled and started for the door. Victor regretted his remark, even though he felt it was obvious that he had made it jokingly.

"Wait a minute, damn it. Don't priss your little ass out of here like that. Come here."

Victor made what was, for him, the considerable concession of standing up and walking around his desk toward the hesitant young brunette. He held out his arms end, after a moment during which she looked at him accusingly through tear-filled eyes, Betty gave a little sob and ran into his arms. She pressed her lush body against him hungrily; he reacted, as always, to the sensual pressure of her large breasts. His hands went around her waist and slipped down to her firm, pliable buttocks.

"Oh, Vic... don't pay any attention to me. I don't know what's wrong with me today – I guess I'm just feeling sorry for myself. Well, I've got my period, for one thing... Anyway, I know you were joking."

Victor breathed a sigh of relief as he stroked the cheeks of her bottom. He was glad she had seen the light without a long explanation of how much she meant to him – even though the explanation would have been true. He was just not in the mood for that sort of foolishness, at the moment...

He pinched one buttock hard enough to make her squeal.

"Okay. Now, if you're straightened out, suppose you send Mrs. O'Connor in. I hope to God *she's* not menstruating; I don't know of a more useless thing than a menstruating woman..."

Betty had at least partially recovered her sense of humour. She reached between their bodies and – pinched his soft penis through his trousers – hard enough to make him wince.

"You bastard. I hope she's 'menstruating' so much she's bleeding out of her mouth too. But I suppose you'd just fuck her in the asshole, wouldn't you?"

But Betty was smiling as she turned her face up to offer her lips for a kiss.

* * *

Victor dropped the application form into the file folder and looked up at the pretty, smartly dressed and obviously nervous woman seated in a chair across from his desk.

"Well, Mrs. O'Connor. You have a good background; good enough for a job as a regular secretary, I think. But this job is not an ordinary one – you understand that, don't you?"

The woman nodded.

"Yes. I'm not sure I understand the whole situation, but your secretary did explain some of the... features of the job."

Victor smiled at the woman's delicate phrasing. In her late twenties, she had the voluptuous figure that was a prerequirement for his position. As he surveyed her he agreed with Betty's evaluation – she had the body if her attitude was right. Well, hell – the sooner he established this the better.

He looked squarely at the woman.

"Alright, I think we should get down to cases. Let me lay it on the line. The real point of this job is that it will involve keeping my customers, and potential customers, happy. And – that means in bed. In short, you'll have to fuck them, and do whatever else they might want, at least within reason. Am I making it perfectly clear?"

To her annoyance, Bridget O'Connor felt herself blushing beet red at his frank language. She hadn't wanted to give anything away, least of all her inherent modesty. She stared at him as though she hardly saw him, and Victor could sense her mental turmoil. He felt a wave of impatience as he began to doubt that this woman was really prepared for a job of this nature. And, damn it, after being told in advance what the requirements were...

"Well, Mrs. O'Connor? I'm waiting for your reply."

The reply was not the one he expected. The nervous woman made an obvious effort to pull herself together.

"I... yes, Mr. Jordan. I understand. You see, I have to have the job... I have to make as much as I can, and I haven't found anything else that pays this much. I... I can do what you want me to..."

Victor studied the woman through skeptical eyes. He just did not think she would go through with it; she was not the type. Still, if she was desperate enough...

"Mrs. O'Connor, you apparently have some rather compelling reasons for taking this job. I don't want to pry into your personal affairs, but I do need to judge your seriousness about the whole thing. Frankly, I get the impression that you're here only as a last resort, and that under normal circumstances you wouldn't even consider a job like this. Am I right?"

The woman seemed to have recovered part of her composure as she looked at him through clearer eyes.

"Yes, you're right. I'm glad it shows; it makes me feel a little better. But I guess it really doesn't matter; I suppose all whores feel they have a good excuse for being what they are. And that is what it amounts to, isn't it? I will be a whore, won't I?"

Victor found himself puzzled, yet intrigued, by the woman's attitude.

"That's a pretty harsh assessment, Mrs. O'Connor. I don't think you have to be that hard on yourself..."

The woman's smile was grim.

"Oh, come on, be honest about it. You want me to entertain men with my body – let them fuck me and do whatever they want to me – and my inducement to do this is money. A little more money than I can make at a regular job. Well, it means that I'm selling my cunt for money... and a woman who does that is a whore, isn't she? Oh, maybe I can consider myself one cut above the woman who lets her customers fuck her in alleys behind bars, if that's any satisfaction..."

Victor found himself increasingly curious about this pretty woman who was obviously engaged in a gigantic struggle with herself.

"Mrs. O'Connor... I get the feeling that you've got some good reason for wanting the extra money. Want to tell me about it? It might help us both for me to understand the situation..."

The woman shrugged with a motion that made her breasts rebound.

"There's not much to tell. It's a pretty typical situation, I guess... a divorce, a sick child, some doctor bills coming up on him, and an ex-husband who won't put in a cent. Oh, I don't want to talk about that. The job – are you going to hire me?"

The question brought Victor's mind back to the practical aspects of the moment. He had about made up his mind that the woman was not suitable, but her story had made him almost change his mind. And she was so damn sexy...

"Well, we're not quite that far along yet. If you're sure you want it, and that you understand clearly what's involved, then the next step is to see how well qualified you are."

The woman looked at him blankly for a moment, then flushed once more as she understood his meaning.

"You mean you want to fuck me, is that it? I believe in second rate novels they call it 'sampling the merchandise'..."

Victor could not restrain a half-leer.

"Well, if you want to put it that way. I'm sure you can understand my point of view – since this is a customer-relation kind of thing I have to be sure that the relations that my customers get will make the right impression..."

The woman was not amused by his weak little joke. She sat with nervous hands twisting in her lap as she looked at him without speaking. Victor could sense that the final round of the battle with her conscience was now taking place. He also knew what the outcome would be.

Her voice was low and her tone indicated a sense of defeat when she finally spoke.

"All right. I'd already made up my mind before I came here; I don't know why I make it harder by going through the whole thing again. I just don't have any choice – that's all there is to it. I... you can fuck me, or whatever it is you want to do."

She paused and looked around the office.

"Are we going to do it here?"

Victor was pleased by her submission and also more interested in sex with her than he had realized. He gestured to the leather-upholstered chaise longue at right angles to his desk.

"Right here, this time. It's not the best place in the world, but I've had some good pussy on that couch."

The woman stared bleakly at the rather worn leather couch.

"I can imagine. Well, do you want me to undress?"

Victor chuckled as he felt his penis twitch at the prospect of seeing her nude body.

"It's best that way. You might open the door and tell my secretary not to bother us before you get naked."

The woman looked at him, and then at the intercom system on his desk. She was perceptive enough to understand that his request was part of his effort to condition her, to subdue her to his will, to break her spirit and foster the correct 'attitude' for the conditions in which she would be operating. Without speaking she rose and moved to the door, giving Victor his best look yet at her supple body. The look confirmed his original impression that she was properly equipped for her new position.

Her words startled Victor as she pulled the heavy door open and spoke to Betty in the outer office.

"Miss... I'm sorry, I don't recall your name. Mr. Jordan wants not to be disturbed. You see, he's going to be busy screwing me."

Victor laughed out loud as the pretty woman closed the door and turned to face him. But the woman did not share his laughter as she looked at him with a serious expression.

"Alright, Mr. Jordan. Do you want me to undress now?"

Victor was still chuckling as he got to his feet and walked over to the standing woman.

"In a minute. I want to feel you a little bit before you take your clothes off."

He moved to her side and ran his eyes down her full figure as he evaluated her body and the way she wore her clothes. He would get a better look at her body when she was nude, but his customers would from their first impression of her while she was fully dressed...

He could see no objection to the initial impression that she made. He knew from her application form that she was twenty eight years old, but neither her age nor the child that she had borne seemed to have had any adverse effects on her figure. Her breasts were large and firmly outhrust, her waist trim and her belly smooth; her hips were softly rounded. He moved a hand up to her bosom and put his fingers lightly on the firm flesh. As he began to caress one breast through her clothes he put the other hand down on a firm buttock and squeezed that enticing flesh.

While fondling the woman, Victor stared into her face. Her eyes avoided his for a moment, then she seemed to realize that this was all a part of her test and she forced herself to look at him and smile. Some genuine amusement came into her smile as she realized that her thoughts had been an open book to him. And his hands did feel good; her experiences with men had been too few and far between lately.

Victor abandoned her bottom and moved around in front of the standing woman. He brought both hands to the mounds of her breasts for a moment, then stepped back slightly.

"Well, Mrs. O'Connor – Bridget, isn't it? Now suppose you undress."

He looked at his watch.

"Hell, we don't have time. I was going to ask for a nice, slow strip, but I have another appointment coming up, so we'll have to hurry this a little. Pretty uncivilized to rush sex, isn't it?"

The woman's mind seemed to be on something other than the need to hurry. She had seen the young girl waiting in the outer office and she knew that the girl's youth would make her a formidable competitor. Bridget O'Connor decided that she had best clinch this job while she had the chance.

And so her reluctance gave way to a sensuality that was almost forceful. She moved toward Victor and looked into his eyes while one of her hands went to the crotch of his trousers and began to stroke the modest bulge she found there.

"I feel something nice. It's not very big yet, but I can take care of that. I bet you have a nice cock, Mr. Jordan. I know my cunt's going to enjoy it."

The woman's words surprised Victor; they represented an almost complete reversal of her previous attitude. Well, whatever the reason, the change was welcome. And effective; she felt his penis surge under her touch.

Bridget leaned forward to bring her face to Victor's. Her little pink tongue flicked out and ran lightly over his closed lips. His reaction was a little slow; by the time his mouth opened to capture her working tongue she backed off with a little pleased laugh.

"Well, Mr. Jordan, looks like I do get to you a little. Frankly, it makes me feel good. I haven't been with many men lately, but I guess that will change now, won't it?"

Victor made no answer as he watched her fingers make fast work of the fasteners on her clothes. In a moment her dress was on the floor around her ankles, and as she stepped out of it he noticed that even the heavy brassiere she wore could not entirely calm the jiggle of her large breasts when she moved. In his self chosen role of connoisseur of the feminine bosom Victor found himself anxious to see her breasts nude.

And his attention did not go unnoticed by Bridget.

"Well, I can see you like them. I think most men do; even my husband, who seemed to lose most of his interest in the rest of me, never seemed to quite get over these. Maybe if I take my bra off you can see why..."

The woman reached behind her back for the catches. In a moment the bra was loose on her chest, but the cups were still smugly encased around their soft contents.

The woman wore a pleased smile as she bent forward and worked the cups off of her breasts with both hands. Finally she let the bra fall to the floor with her dress. When she straightened up her hands held the heavy mounds in a gesture that was simultaneously protective and provocative

Then the protective element faded as her hands began to fondle the big globes in a manner that was intensely erotic. Victor could see her nipples harden under the action of her own fingers.

He drew a deep breath and shifted slightly as his erect penis became uncomfortably cramped in the confinement of his trousers.

"You've got me pretty worked up here, Bridget, and my pants are getting a little tight. How about helping me out? After all, it's your fault..."

The woman laughed softly.

"I guess it is, isn't it? Okay, I'll see what I can do. Your prick felt good while ago when it wasn't even hard..."

The pretty divorcee paused and looked up into his face.

"You know, it's funny... I never have used language like this before. These words, I mean – even to my husband. But I guess if I'm going to do the things it won't hurt much more to talk about them will it?"

Victor's arousal precluded much interest in philosophical questions.

"I wouldn't think so. But right now let's concentrate on my prick. Wouldn't want him to choke to death."

Bridget laughed again.

"No, that's no way for your cock to die. Of course he may drown in my cunt. It's already wet... Here, let me see!"

She was standing close to him now, nude except for brief panties, garter belt and hose. Both of her small hands went to Victor's bulge for a moment, then she attacked his zipper and in another moment she had his erect penis out of his clothes and was rolling it gently in her hands.

"My... Mr. Jordan, it *is* handsome. It's funny – I never thought of a man's penis before quite the way I'm thinking about yours. Maybe I've got a different outlook about it now that I'm going to... to fuck for money. Or maybe I just haven't had enough lately, I don't know... anyway, your penis... prick seems nice. Awfully nice. And from the way it feels I think it's a little interested in me, too..."

Victor's hands were back on her nude breasts as she fondled his penis.

"More than just a little. You've got me hot as hell. Tell you what – you slip your panties off while I strip. We can play another time – right now I need action. But first give it a little kiss. My prick likes to be kissed. Then we'll fuck."

His words made the woman stiffen, but in his arousal Victor did not notice it. His request that she kiss his penis was, under the circumstances, not surprising, and Bridget recognized this. Nevertheless, the request did trigger a fresh wave of anxiety and doubt. She stalled, holding his penis in both hands as she looked down at the hard shaft. Damn, why did she have to be so sensitive about this particular thing? It was an act which she had enjoyed and at which she had been highly proficient in the early days of her marriage. She had known, at least subconsciously, that it would be part of the required repertoire for this job, but apparently she had never really come to grips with that fact during her tortured decision making processes. Well, she was face to face with it now, and there could be no further avoidance of the issue. And, hell – morally, what was the difference whether a man ejaculated into her vagina or her mouth?

She felt Victor's hands leave her breasts and go to her shoulders to exert a gentle but firm downward pressure. "Go on, baby. Suck it for a minute, then we'll fuck on the couch. I'm not gonna come in your mouth this time. Hurry up..."

The trance like feeling that she had overcome earlier enveloped Bridget again as she allowed herself to sink to her knees in front of him. She looked again at his penis, now immediately in front of her face; and tried to steel herself for the coming ordeal. She felt his fingers in her hair behind her head and she knew that they would exert a pressure if she did not quickly accept his penis.

She stared at the organ as one of her hands continued to grasp its base. Her hesitation was not based on a physical repugnance; on the contrary she had, in the past, found this act to be a particularly satisfying one. But that had been with her husband, during the happy part of their marriage. This penis belonged to a man whom she did not really even know, much less have any real feeling for. And yet it had to be done...

"Bridget, baby... come on, honey. Give it a nice little suck. Then I want your cunt..."

The woman closed her eyes and forced her head forward. She felt the head of his organ brush her lips, and she instinctively turned her head to avoid the contact. In an effort to conceal her feelings she rubbed the hard and yet velvet surface of Victor's penis on her cheek as she reached again into his trousers and withdrew the wrinkled sac of his testicles.

Bridget continued to rub his erection on her cheek as her other hand fondled the mounds in the loose sac she held. She did feel a little of the old physical reaction that her husband's penis had given her, but she also sensed that her response in this would, and could, go no farther. And yet she would have to make herself do it. She opened her mouth and took the head of his penis inside.

Victor sighed in pleasure as he felt her

acceptance of his penis in her warm, wet mouth. His physical arousal prevented any subtle awareness of the nuances of that acceptance, and he rather roughly hunched forward to thrust more of his shaft into the woman's mouth.

Suppressing her desire to gag, she took the big, velvety plum of his glans far back into her mouth until it touched the back of her throat. She relaxed still more, and even succeeded in taking it deeper, so that her oesophagus began to squeeze it gently. Bridget's eyes were watering, and as he withdrew, she smiled to herself in secret triumph: he had not come in her mouth, it was true, yet she felt as if she had overcome her irrational phobia of tasting male sperm.

"OK, quick now, kneel on the couch, with your ass up high."

The tone of Victor's voice brooked no hesitation. Bridget quickly conformed to his request and assumed what is possibly the most humiliating position that a naked woman can present to a relative stranger: she knelt, thrusting her shapely bottom out and up, cradling her head in her folded arms, acutely aware that her entire crotch was indecently displayed to this powerful man.

"My, my, Mrs. O'Connor. That's a damned fine ass you've got there."

Bridget flinched as Victor slid the middle finger of his upturned hand into the groove of her cunt, while the fingers of his other hand mauled her left breast and cruelly pinched its big, erect nipple. Opening the thick inner lips of her vagina, he could feel her eager wetness gush from within. He jammed two of his fingers deep into her vagina. Startled by this uncompromising approach to one of the most sensitive parts of her body, Bridget let out a groan of near-pain mingled with unaccustomed physical pleasure.

"Mmm… and it seems like you're ready for a good fuck, too.

Now she could feel his velvety-smooth cock head parting her hairy outer lips until it lodged at the entrance to her cunt. Oh god, why doesn't he just shove it in… please, *just do it now*! she thought. But instead he lingered, tantalising her further, with big glans nestling just inside the entrance to her vaginal tunnel.

When he slammed his solid rod into her, it was with a thrust so ferocious that it nearly winded her. He pulled out and shoved his cock back in again even harder so that her big, heavy breasts swung like bells. Then he started fucking her in earnest. Her body was buffeted by each powerful in-thrust as his loins smacked up against her luscious posterior globes with a loud report. Again, he reached forwards with both hands and grabbed her lovely pendulous breasts, squeezing and mauling them until she groaned, this time with pure, unadulterated lust. Victor's strong fingers pinched her suffused nipples, quickly bringing the lovely divorcee to a high pitch of exquisite, agonising, pleasure.

"You like it doggie-fashion, Mrs. O'Connor?

Are you going to be a good bitch for your master?"

Red-faced, Bridget nodded her head and moaned a 'yes', thrusting back at him. She was so nearly there... what did it matter if he wanted to humiliate her? Ohh... if only she could come – it had been such a long time since...

But it was not to be. Victor pulled his dripping cock out of her wet, clasping cunt. A heady odour of sex hung heavily in the air.

"That's enough, Bridget. Anyone can fuck. Now let's see how well you suck."

She felt his hands in her hair begin to turn her face back squarely toward his loins. Again the head of his hardness rubbed over her lips, and again she could not bring herself to open those lips...

"Come on, honey. What gives? You having some second thoughts? Sorry, baby, but you've got to suck my prick, and others, if you want this job..."

His words were the expected ones. Hell, the decision had been made, she'd already sucked his cock and her stalling now would only making it worse... Bridget stifled a sob and forced her reluctant lips to open and spread around the head of the throbbing organ.

Her eyes were still closed as she felt his penis penetrate her mouth and make contact with the back of her throat and far beyond. She began to gag; she had never been able to take a penis this far into her mouth without problems. But she made an honest effort; her tongue and lips caressed the hard shaft and she tried to begin a series of short bobbing motions with her head to move her mouth on his penis in a simulation of the strokes of love.

And her effort might have been successful, but Victor inadvertently killed the chances when his passion got the best of him. His body began to tremble and his fingers tangled in her hair as she heard him mumble far above her working head. "Baby, I'm gettin' too close. Didn't mean to come this way, but… Honey, I got to finish – I'm gonna come in your mouth. Suck it, baby – suck my prick. Damn…"

But his words had an unexpected effect on the woman on her knees before him with his penis in her reluctant mouth. She would not – could not – permit him to climax in her mouth. He had asked her to suck his organ only as a prelude to conventional sex, and now he was changing the ground rules in the middle of the game – now he wanted to spurt his disgusting, thick sperm into her mouth. She would not do it – she could not make herself do it. It was beside the point to tell herself that she had already agreed to do it, that this was no worse than it would be later on with the clients. And the fact that she already had his penis in her mouth meant nothing. The simple fact was that she could not take his ejaculation in her mouth…

Bridget rocked slowly back on her knees and let his throbbing penis slip from between her lips. One of her hands was still on it as she turned her wet face up to look at him. "I... Mr. Jordan, I'm sorry. I just... I can't do it. I thought I could, but I can't. I'm sorry..."

Anger flooded over Victor as his lust saturated brain finally understood her refusal. Damn prick teaser – get him all worked up and then back out...

But the tears in her eyes as she knelt in front of him and looked up with anguish in her face erased part of his anger. He sensed that she had made a sincere effort to go through with it. But effort was not enough; he needed release. Hell...

The nude woman struggled to her feet as tears streamed down her cheeks. "I'm sorry. I shouldn't even have come here, but I thought... I'm just not the right person for the job, Mr. Jordan." Her wet eyes went to his waving, painfully hard erection. "I... I'll make you come with my hand, if you want me to. But that's all I can do – I'm sorry."

Victor considered her offer briefly, but he wanted more than manual stimulation. Then suddenly he thought of the other applicant waiting for her interview. A young girl – perhaps not as inhibited as this woman...

"Never mind, Mrs. O'Connor. I understand; no hard feelings. But I do have a little problem, and maybe the other girl can help me with it. I wonder if you'd mind gathering up your clothes and going into that room to dress." He pointed to the door to an adjoining office that was vacant at the moment. "I imagine that you agree that there's not much else to discuss. Perhaps we can employ you on a freelance basis sometimes, you never know. Occasionally we get a big group of clients to entertain."

Bridget nodded as she stooped to pick up her clothes. She seemed to feel a little better, and she realized that her decision had restored at least a part of her self-respect. She managed a small, tight smile as she turned to leave the room with her clothes in her arms. "I agree, Mr. Jordan. No hard feelings. And of course, if the pay is good, I'd be pleased to help you out." But though the sight of the man standing fully dressed but with his erect penis and testicles absurdly exposed was an exact metaphor for what he was – an arrogant, selfish prick, she was furious. Bridget O'Connor had not finished with this man. Nobody behaved towards her like that and got away with it. He would suffer the consequences of treating her with such patronising contempt. She opened the door and was gone.

Victor stared stupidly at the door for a moment, then absently rubbed his penis with one hand as he moved to his desk and leaned over to punch the intercom.

"Betty – is the girl out there? Okay, send her in. What? No – Mrs. O'Connor is not suitable. She'll be leaving through the other office. Betty – this kid look okay? I don't want another dry run… Good. Alright, have her come in. What's her name? Yeah… okay."

Victor clicked the intercom off and then faced the door, still leaning on his desk. A vague thought that he probably presented a ludicrous sight with his prick and balls hanging out crossed his mind, but he didn't give a damn. The other broad had worked him up to the point that nothing mattered except to get his rocks off in a female some way or another…

Victor was suddenly aware that he was staring at a cute miniskirted young girl who was in turn staring at him with wide eyes. She recovered first; a peal of feminine laughter came from the almost tiny blonde.

"Mr. Jordan, you… you look like you're in bad shape. Did the other applicant leave you like that? Wow – your cock looks like it's ready to pop. And that's okay with me as long as it pops in my pussy. Boy – I knew this job involved fucking, but I didn't know it would start *quite* so soon. Well, I can't think of a better way to begin…"

Victor grinned wolfishly at the girl. She was obviously the answer to his present problem, and very likely the girl for the job. She was extremely young, but a quick survey of her small body showed no deficiencies – only assets. And, most important, her attitude seemed to be right…

"Glad to hear you talk like that, Jill. Jill Feinberg, isn't it? As you so astutely noticed,

I do have a little problem here. Think you can solve it for me? We can take care of the other part of the interview afterward. How about just coming on over here…"

The young girl did not have to be coaxed. With an expression that seemed to include about equal parts of amusement, curiosity, and simple lust, she moved close to him as he continued to lean back against the edge of his desk. Her eyes were on his penis, and she reached out and touched the end of it with the tip of one finger. The touch was mild but somehow tremendously suggestive, and Victor felt his arousal escalate another notch. Damn, he'd shoot on the carpet yet if he wasn't careful…

The girl rubbed the little orifice in the tip of his organ for a moment, then raised the finger so that they could both see the glistening wetness that it had acquired. Then she brought the finger to her lips and into her mouth as she sampled the fluid from his penis. The gesture was simple but erotic and made Victor cup her cheeks in his hands as she slowly pulled her finger out of her mouth and smiled at him.

He grinned back, feeling slightly foolish but not caring. This girl, who looked like she should be in school instead of in his office teasing his penis, was exactly what he needed at the moment…

"Jill… Jill, I guess this is a little abrupt, but I need to fuck you. Right now. We'll get to details later; in any case you won't regret it.

Sound okay to you?"

The girl smiled and nodded. "It's okay with me, Mr. Jordan. I knew this was a fuck job, although I didn't know it would start exactly like this. But I'm all for it." She paused and looked around the room. "How do you want me? Want me to kneel down and suck you off right there?"

Victor considered the offer, which was attractive but somehow not exactly what he wanted at the moment. What did he want…?

His eyes fell on a low, straight chair by his desk.

"Jill – we'll make this a quickie and take a good slow fuck later. Pull your skirt up and take your panties off and lean over that chair – I think the arms are about the right height. Or maybe you'll want to put your elbows and forearms on the seat. Anyway, I'll fuck you from behind, dog fashion. I mean your cunt, not your asshole. We'll get to that later, but right now I don't want to take the time to go slow, and all that. Sound okay?"

The young girl smiled up at him as she again reached for his penis, this time to capture it in the full grip of both of her small hands. She began to rotate it gently between her palms as she started a simultaneous stroking motion.

"Sounds okay to me. To tell the truth, I sat outside thinking about you fucking that other broad in here and I got hot as hell. I bet my panties are soaked. I'm glad I've got a juicy cunt, but there are times..."

"Yeah, I know. Right now I'm about to have a juicy prick."

Victor's hands covered the girl's and stilled their motion on his penis.

"No more of that, baby – I'm too close. Come on, slip your panties off and bend over that chair – I want to fuck."

The girl giggled as she complied. A petite, copper-haired redhead, the girl seemed to be no older than about seventeen. But her body was complete, and Victor, usually a devotee of lushness in the female figure, found himself intrigued by the girl's slender build.

He was really much too aroused to appreciate the subtleties of the feminine body at the moment. He needed relief, and almost any woman who was reasonably attractive would serve his immediate needs...

The girl moved quickly as she sensed that this was not the time for delay. She raised her miniskirt high enough to slip off her bikini panties, and she continued to hold the skirt above her pubic mound after the panties were on the floor.

"Like me? I'm a real redhead, as you can see. I hope you like a red-haired pussy, 'cos I won't bleach it. I have a girl friend who tried that, and she got so sore she couldn't fuck for two weeks. I don't think you'd want that to happen to me."

"No, I wouldn't. Jill, baby – less yakking

and more fucking, huh? Come on, honey, over the chair..."

The girl laughed again as she bent over the chair that Victor indicated. Immediately he saw that the position was unworkable; the little redhead was small enough for their heights to be incompatible for what was, essentially, a standing position...

"Damn. It's not gonna work, honey."

Victor looked around the room and then back at the chair.

"Come on, let's see you sit on my prick. You like to do that?"

She nodded hard.

Jill watched him as he quickly sat down on the chair and stretched out so that his body was almost in a straight line. Victor was still fully dressed except for his genital exposure, but the sight was no longer funny to the girl because her own growing arousal made sexual relief an increasing necessity for her, too...

"Okay, sweet – straddle me and sit on my prick. Glad your cunt is wet, because I don't intend to fuck around – or maybe that's exactly what I am gonna do. That's it... comfortable? Let your cunt down on my prick. You hold it and guide it. Easy... God, baby, don't try to bend it. It's so hard it's brittle – you'll break it off."

The young girl was now on top of Victor with her legs spread across his as she reached under her crotch to grasp his penis and hold it in position.

"If it does break off can I have it? I'll just put it up my pussy and leave it there. The best dildo yet... oh, God – that feels good. Mr Jordan, you sure stuff my cunt full. I think it's coming up my throat..."

Victor did not answer the eager girl. His eyes were closed as he enjoyed every progressive millimetre of his penis' entry into her tight, juicy sheath. He was very close now, and he knew that his pleasure would be short, so he hesitated to begin a stroking motion...

But the girl was not hesitant. Her own arousal demanded relief, and she paused only briefly after the initial penetration before she began to move her loins in a stroking motion that caused her tight vagina to move sensuously over the length of his shaft. Her position was awkward, almost uncomfortable, but the results were more than satisfactory for both of them.

And then, unexpectedly, her movement ceased. Victor opened startled eyes and finally made them focus on the girl's smiling but intent face.

"What the hell, baby? Don't stop humping now... keep going you horny little bitch!"

Jill leaned forward and kissed him lightly without resuming her motion. "Oh, I will, lover, just as soon as you tell me what I want to hear. I need this fuck as bad as you do, but I need the job, too – I *am* hired, aren't I?"

Victor laughed, not unpleasantly.

"You little prick teaser. Yes, damn it, you've

got the job – provided you get that little ass of yours back to work and make me come before I change my mind..."

Her hips were already in motion again. "No problem, boss. You just stay still and let little Jill fuck that big thing of yours. If you don't like the way I make you come I won't take the job..."

The girl was hired.

Chapter 3

Mary was silent as she stared at her son-in-law. His request had caught her by surprise; she had not been prepared for the sort of thing that he asked of her. And she had very little choice; if she objected it could cause serious problems just as he and Jessie were leaving on their honeymoon...

Victor looked up from the bar at the lovely woman who was his wife's mother.

"You're not very responsive, Mary. I had hoped you wouldn't object – you have to understand that I'm asking you to do it only because it is sort of an emergency. The girls that I usually use for this kind of thing are not available tonight for one reason or another. Hell, I hired a girl permanently a couple of days ago to take care of my customers but she's already booked up for tonight. These two just came in unexpectedly and I didn't have a chance to make any plans. But they represent an outfit that sells stationery to department stores in six states and I can't afford to lose their business. Mary, darling, I don't like to ask you, but I just don't have any alternative. I want you to understand that..."

Mary sighed; she knew that he knew that she could not refuse. It was this, as much as anything that she resented.

"Oh Victor, I... well, I want to be cooperative, but I'm not used to things like this. What... I mean, what exactly would they expect?"

Victor laughed in a way that seemed almost humourless as he searched beneath the bar for ice.

"Damn, I thought sure we had ice... Well, hell, Mary... sometimes you're more naive than Jessie. They expect sex, of course. I don't know their detailed preferences, but your abilities should be varied enough to handle the situation. They may not want anything but straight fucking. I'm sorry I haven't got another girl to send with you, but that's the way it is. I don't feel like asking Jessie to go, right before we start our honeymoon. I'm sure you can understand that..."

Mary found herself increasingly shocked by his cavalier manner. It had never occurred to her that he would ask such a thing even of her. Now he had implied that only special circumstances prevented him from considering his wife for such a task. Damn, she had known Victor was pretty far out in his sexual thinking, but this was more than she had bargained for... Had she made a mistake when she had conceived this whole plan, this arrangement under which she as well as Jessie was available physically to this man? Certainly she had never dreamed that he would consider his privileges transferable to his business customers...

But the issue was never really in doubt, and they both knew it. Victor smiled confidently as he tossed off the rest of his drink and picked up a little pad from a shelf behind the apartment's tiny bar. He scribbled on the paper for a moment, then tore off a sheet and held it toward Mary.

"Better take this so there won't be any foul-up. And don't be late; you've got less than an hour..."

* * *

Mary's mind was still angry and confused as she spotted the motel two blocks ahead. She slowed the new Thunderbird in an unconscious effort to delay her arrival as much as possible and was rewarded by an impatient horn blast behind her. But she was not even aware of the other driver; her thoughts were focused grimly on her present situation and the larger implications that it brought up. It was probably true that Victor would not have asked this of her under normal circumstances, at least not quite this soon, but the whole thing made his basic outlook uncomfortably clear. Mary's desire for Victor and Jessie's marriage, so strong a few weeks ago, now began to seem like a possibly monumental miscalculation. And yet she could not afford to question the whole situation too soon. Besides, maybe this was an exception.

Mary was startled by the realization that she had already entered the motel grounds. She stared dumbly at the crowd of children at one of the motel's two pools, then turned her face away from the noisy group with the realization that it would be best not to be recognized. She drove past the pool into an area that was growing dark in the gathering dusk and stopped the car to fish nervously in her purse for the slip of paper Victor had given her. She found it and looked at the number on it, then up at the nearest room number.

Mary let out a little startled cry as the ground's lighting system came on and destroyed the slight sense of privacy she had felt in the gloom. She lurched the car forward as she tried to decipher the room numbering system...

* * *

Mary crossed her legs and watched the men's eyes go to the flesh of her thighs, which was shown to advantage by her skirt. The subject of their interest was obvious, but at least they were younger and less unattractive than the mental image she had had... And they seemed to be pleased by her appearance.

The youngest, a man apparently under forty and with only a hint of a paunch, spoke in a voice that was obviously intended to put their pretty visitor at ease.

"Well Mary, I'm glad it worked out this way. I... well, I have to say that I wasn't too happy when Victor told me he was sending his mother-in-law, but I had no idea that his wife had such a lovely mother. Victor's wife must be awfully young..."

The other man, fifty-ish, definitely paunchy and balding, but maybe the better looking of the two, laughed a little too loudly.

"Yeah, she probably is pretty young."

He grinned at the younger man.

"We'll probably get to find out sooner or later; Jordan hinted that he'd have sent her this time except they were leaving on their honeymoon. How 'bout that? We'll probably get to fuck his wife later on. And right now his mother-in-law, of all people, looks like a pretty good piece of ass to me..."

Mary sucked in a sharp breath as the import of their words hit her. Not only were the men as crude as she had first feared, but Victor's unwarranted frankness with them held a grim promise for the future...

"... hear me, baby? I asked you if your daughter is a good fuck. I bet she is if she's got a body like yours. Say, does Victor fuck you too?

I bet he does, from the way he talked. What about it, honey?"

Mary looked blankly at the men, appalled by their unnecessary vulgarity. Damn them, they didn't have to talk this way.

But even the younger man's conversation was suddenly lewd.

"Hey, Eddie – you know what? I bet we could have a party and fuck both of 'em at once. Mother and daughter at the same time – on the same bed so everybody can watch everybody fuck. How 'bout that? You ever done anything like that?"

The older man grinned as his eyes stayed on Mary's legs.

"Yeah, a long time ago. Stayed in a hotel in Tijuana where this maid sneaked her daughter in for the men. Only charged five bucks, and the two of 'em would do anything you wanted. Used to have one suck my prick while the other stuck her tongue up my ass... then I'd fuck one and have the other one suck my come out of her pussy."

He paused and seemed to consider.

"Course a dollar was worth something in those days..."

The younger man laughed.

"Yeah, prices have gone up quite a bit since World War One. But, what the hell – this fucking won't cost us a thing."

Then he turned back to Mary.

"Hey, baby, you never did answer the

question. Does Victor fuck you?"

Mary stared at him as she tried to keep her feelings from showing. She was mad, but Victor was the real culprit, and it would only make things worse to antagonize these men.

"Let's not worry about other people; let's just think about what we're going to do. What do you boys like?"

Neither man pressed the question. The older man, who seemed to be his companion's superior, chuckled as his eyes continued to rove over Mary's figure. He seldom looked at her face.

"Well now, honey, we're not too particular. We do like variety. Apart from your exotic, oriental pussy, what you got to offer?"

Mary made herself continue the preposterous conversation as the thought struck her that this was probably the standard whore – customer routine. Well, why not? There was no other way to accurately classify her function here... and for that matter maybe she had really made a whore out of herself when she made the deal with Victor in the first place. Certainly he seemed to see it in that light...

The younger man seemed displeased.

"Mary, you got a hell of a habit of ignoring somebody when they talk to you. Eddie asked you a question, and you just sit there."

"Sorry. I... my mind's kind of wandering, I guess. This is the first time I... I've done anything like this, and I'm a little nervous."

The older man spoke.

"Yeah, I think that's the truth, Bill. Don't bitch at her; I think Suzie Wong here's gonna be real sweet to us. That right, honey?"

"That's right. You won't have any complaints."

Although she was stung by the older man's racist quip, Mary decided to cooperate fully and get this distasteful episode over as quickly as possible. Then she would have a chance to re-evaluate the whole situation, but in the meantime she could not afford to make any hasty decisions. And, since it had to be done, she might as well make it as pleasant as possible for the men and herself. It had been a long time since she had dealt with two men at once...

Mary decided to get the activities underway.

"Well, boys, maybe you'd like to see what Victor's giving you. Would you like me to undress?"

Both men grinned.

"Hell yes. I'm ready to fuck. Let's get this show on the road."

The younger man turned to his associate.

"How you want to work it, Eddie? You want me to go in the other room to start with?"

The older man seemed disgusted.

"Not unless you're bashful about the way you fuck. I'm sure as hell not. Let's have the little lady undress and play with us a little, then we'll decide what to do. My problem is that I'm at the stage where I can't usually come but once a night, so I don't wanna waste it. At your age you oughta be good for three comes, anyway."

The other man grinned.

"Usually. Except with my wife. You know, it's a funny thing – Estelle can get me hot the first time as quick as any female in the country, but I've got to where I can hardly even fuck her twice. But when I've got a broad like Mary, I can usually screw her three times, and maybe more. It's hard to figure – I guess it's just that a man gets so used to his wife. Hell, I hope I don't get to where I have trouble fuckin' her the first time..."

Eddie smiled faintly, but he seemed to have little real interest in his companion's marital situation. His eyes were still locked on Mary, and now he beckoned to her.

"Come on, baby – let's see what you got. I can already see it's gonna be good..."

Mary felt a slight sense of relief as she stood up and prepared to undress for the men. She did not want to expose her body to them, but since it had to be done there was a certain secondary satisfaction in the activity involved. It seemed easier than just sitting there subject to their lewd looks and remarks...

Mary wore a smart, low cut dress. She pivoted to let them see her back and bottom, then reached behind herself to pull the dress' zipper while her back was to them. She heard a mild exclamation from one of them as the plunging "V" of her bare skin revealed by the opening fastener showed that she had bothered with neither bra nor panties.

"Hot Damn! I thought from the way her tits wiggled she didn't have on no bra. You know, I made Estelle go to a dance without a bra awhile back, but nothing much happened. I guess her tits are a little too small to bounce the way Mary's do under her dress. Turn around, honey, and let's have a squint at those boobies..."

Mary worked the dress off her shoulders as she pivoted. She could not help but be pleased at the obvious impact of her nude breasts on the two men as she faced them squarely.

"There they are, boys. I hope you like them – sometimes I worry that they're just a little *too* big..."

As she teased them Mary brought her hands up to cup the heavy mounds. She began to fondle and knead the firm flesh as she watched the men's reaction. Finally her fingers moved to her dark tan nipples and quickly completed their arousal; in a minute the little buds were erect and sensitive even to her gentle touch.

"There – my nipples are hard. Can you tell from there? It's a shame that a girl has to play with her own tits to get her nipples hard. But I guess some men just aren't interested in a girl's boobs..."

Eddie grinned at Mary's teasing.

"Yeah, you are havin' a hard time, sweetheart. Tell you what – suppose you march that little ass of yours over here and we'll see what we can do. Maybe we can help you a little."

Mary pretended to hesitate, then she walked slowly to the couch on which they both sat. She moved in between the couch and the coffee table which was now covered with glasses and beer cans and came to a halt between the two men. Her hands were still on her breasts, and she rubbed her hard nipples again and then once more cupped the heavy mounds in her palms and held them out toward the men.

"Here – I've done all I can with them. It's up to you now to make them feel better..."

The men seemed willing to accept their responsibility. Each took a breast and began to fondle it with eager hands. Their eagerness was, in fact, a little too pronounced.

"Hey! Boys... be gentle. Don't maul them. Titties should be handled gently. There... that's better. Oh, that feels good. Do you like my boobies?"

Mary got no verbal answer; both men had been seized with a simultaneous desire to sample her breasts orally. The sight of the beautiful, mature oriental woman standing before the two seated men while they sucked her nipples like hungry infants might have had humorous overtones to a disinterested spectator, but these three people involved were far from disinterested. The libido of all concerned was responding wildly to the sensual situation...

Mary was no less affected than the men. Her beautiful almond eyes narrowed in pure enjoyment of the delightful sensations she was experiencing and she rolled her pretty head back while her hands went to the heads of the men to press their working mouths even more firmly to her sensitive bosom.

"Oh, God... that feels good. I love to have my tits sucked – and it's divine to have them both sucked at once..."

But the men, enthralled as they were by the lush bosom, had other things in mind. The older man was the first to draw his face away from Mary's wet breast.

"Okay, Mary, we've worked on you – now you work on us. Drop down here between us and get our pricks out. We'll show you what we're gonna give you."

Mary was more than willing. She had accomplished the considerable task of putting all of her doubts and fears out of her mind for the time being, and this left the pleasant subject of physical gratification as her only current concern.

And the sex organs of the two men were vital to the gratification. Mary's eyes were wide with expectation as she sank to her knees between the men and reached for the interesting bulges which were visible in the trousers of each. Her soft fingers closed on the bulges and she found herself pleased by the conditions that the bulges represented.

"Oh yes! I think you both have lovely pricks. They feel so nice – they're hard already, and I haven't even got them out yet. But I will..."

The aroused woman quickly pulled the zippers on the men's trousers. Then, as she kneeled between them, her hands went into their clothes and found both organs of pleasure. She grasped them firmly and began to squeeze and pump them without bringing them out of the trousers.

It quickly became apparent to Mary that her initial impression of their arousal was not entirely correct. To her surprise she found that the penis of the younger man, though large, was still fairly soft. Finally she brought both organs out into view as her hands continued to fondle them.

"They are nice. Eddie, you're already hard enough to fuck me. Bill, honey, I'll have to give you a little something extra..."

The significance of her remark did not escape the older man and he suddenly looked over at his companion's organ as Mary's hand continued to caress it.

"What the hell, Bill, is the old man gettin' ahead of you? Hell, I got twenty years on you and a pretty girl can still get me hard quicker than you."

The man rocked with almost silent laughter.

"Hell boy, maybe you need a little help with Estelle."

The younger man grinned weakly as Mary continued to masturbate both of them.

"Don't worry about it, Bill. I can take care of the home front. For that matter, I can take care of Mary, too. Want to put a little money on how many times each of us can come?"

Eddie's laughter subsided gradually.

"I guess not – I know my limits. But looks like I do get worked up faster than you do..."

Mary took over in an effort to keep the situation on an even keel.

"You did get hard a little faster, Eddie, but Bill has about caught up. The fact is both of you have lovely cocks. Either one of you can be proud of it. I don't imagine your wives ever complain...

"No, not usually. Mary baby, suck it a little. I want you to suck my prick a little, then we'll undress. I guess to keep it even you ought to suck Bill's a little, too – if it's hard enough, that is..."

The younger man laughed, secure now in the knowledge that his organ was erect, and was likely to remain that way much longer than the older man's. But he had no objection to the suggestion ..

"Suits me. Go on, baby. Take his prick first. Age before beauty, and all that..."

Mary found herself curiously willing to proceed. This was without doubt the lewdest thing she had ever done – nude to the waist, she knelt between two men whom she barely knew as she fondled their organs preparatory to taking them in her mouth – but she was herself aroused and surprisingly eager to comply with their demands...

"All right, boys. I... I don't mind sucking your pricks. I've never done it before – not like this, I mean – but I don't really mind. I bet your pricks taste good..."

Mary's voice trailed off as she leaned toward the older man with her eyes on the tip of his erect penis above the grasp of her white hand. She slowed her hand's pumping motion and stared at the clear liquid that she had caused to come out of the little piss-slit at the top of his penis...

Then her face was at the hard organ and she turned slightly to rub it on one soft cheek. She faced it squarely again and kissed it lightly with warm but closed lips. After a moment her mouth opened to reveal a pink, wet tongue which first licked her own lips and then flicked out to make contact with the man's penis.

The contact made both people quiver. Mary closed her eyes as she took the organ deeper into her warm mouth and began to suck gently on it. The man groaned in pleasure as he also closed his eyes and rolled his head back against the couch. Mary's working mouth began to make little wet noises as she sucked...

And the younger man was by no means left out of the sensual tableau. His eyes were open and locked on Mary's face and mouth even as one of her hands continued to pull and stroke his penis. Her tempo on his organ was set by the rhythm of her head as it began a bobbing motion on the organ between her lips. She was aware of the old feeling in her own unattended crotch; still covered by the lower part of her dress, her vagina was becoming wet and beginning to throb.

And then the evening's first chapter was ended by the man who was profiting most from it. Eddie put his hands in Mary's short black bob and gently lifted her face from his crotch.

"We better let up, baby. I may get hard faster than Bill the first time, but the second time would be something else. I want to make my first come a long one, because it'll probably be my only one. And I can't take much of that little mouth of yours without shootin' in it.."

Mary stared at him somewhat stupidly as her lust filled mind had trouble following him. But her attention was quickly diverted.

"Well, I haven't got no problems, baby. Come over here and see how Bill's prick tastes… If you want a load of come I'll give it to you. Don't wanna brag, but I've been told that my come's got about the best flavour of anybody's. Used to have a girl who'd jack me off and catch the come in a jar so she could save it to eat when I was gone."

Bill's tale of the remarkable qualities of his semen failed to amuse Mary. Her eyes had homed in on his penis, and her immediate goal was the limited one of using it as a replacement for the organ she had just lost.

The beautiful 38-year-old shifted her kneeling position slightly as she leaned toward the younger man. One of her hands remained on the other man's penis but her grip was a stationary one in deference to his high state of arousal and the consequences of a premature ejaculation.

Again Mary lowered her face to a man's waiting crotch and again her tongue flicked out to make contact with his penis. This time her attack was more direct; her arousal precluded some of the teasing subtleties that she had used on the older man.

But if Bill noticed the difference he did not seem concerned. In any case he would have found it hard to complain as Mary's expert and willing mouth found its own stimulation as it held and drew on the man's erection. Mary's position was increasingly uncomfortable; on her knees with her dress twisted around her hips, her pussy needed attention that she could not immediately give it. She was tempted to use her own fingers in it for temporary relief, but she sensed that abandonment of either of the hard organs would bring a protest. And so she wiggled to rub her hairy outer labia together slightly while she continued to concentrate on her primary task of pleasing her clients. The thought flicked through her mind that if she was a whore she lacked professionalism; it was undoubtedly amateurish to let her own desires get so nearly out of control.

The man on whose penis Mary's mouth worked stared down at her bobbing head through weary eyes as his hands rested lightly in her hair. He too, in spite of his boasts about his ability to achieve multiple orgasms, was concerned about a premature climax. And Mary's warm lips and tongue were bringing his orgasm closer by the second. His first inclination was to let nature take its course and provide Mary's mouth with his first offering of semen, but he had enough judgment still functioning to realize that this would be short sighted.

And so, reluctantly, he came to the same decision that the older man had reached.

"Mary... baby, that's enough. Let's break it off before I come..."

His hands tangled in Mary's already dishevelled hair to halt the motion of her lips on his penis.

The distraught woman felt deprived for a second time. While ordinarily she would have been extremely reluctant to permit either of these men to ejaculate in her mouth, in her present state of perverse arousal she actually resented their refusal to climax between her lips.

Angrily she drew back from Bill's organ and looked up at him with flashing eyes.

"What's wrong with you? Both of you... you want me to suck your damn pricks but you don't want to finish. Talk about prick-teasers... you two tease with your pricks..."

The older man, at the moment the most rational person in the room, laughed as he leaned over to caress Mary's cheek even as her hand continued to grasp his penis.

"Mary, take it easy. We're gonna give you all the loving you want. If you want to take some come in your mouth I'll see that you get it. But it is best for us not to shoot so quick."

He paused as he considered the pleasant problem.

"Of course we don't want to go too far the other way, either... we're all three worked up and we ought to go ahead..."

He looked at his companion, who still had his hands in Mary's hair as she knelt between them.

"Bill boy, let's go in the bedroom and do this right. What say we give her a double fuck – in her cunt and asshole at the same time?"

The younger man finally took one hand out of Mary's hair to wipe away the sweat that had collected on his brow in spite of the motel's efficient air conditioning.

"Well, we can try it. But I'll tell you – I don't think double fucking is what it's cracked up to be. It sounds fine, but it never works too good. Somebody always winds up being uncomfortable as hell. I'd just as soon as do a fuck-suck deal if you're hot on a combination. Or I'll try the double fuck if you want to..."

Eddie shook his head.

"No, you're right – it usually doesn't turn

out too hot. The other suits me okay. Which end of her you want?"

Bill grinned.

"You take your choice. Like I said, age before beauty.

The older man grinned back.

"Alright, kiddo. I'll give you her mouth and I'll take her ass. That'll give me a choice of her pussy or asshole..."

The subject of their conversation had listened with impatience. She released their organs and struggled to stand up on somewhat unsteady legs.

"Okay, if you two have decided what you want to do to me, let's have it. My pussy's so wet I can feel it running down my leg. Let's go to bed and have a little action instead of so much talk. Maybe you'd like to see my cunt..."

As she spoke Mary pulled the other zipper on her and allowed it to finish its interrupted journey down her body. When it reached the floor she stood nude except for garter belt and hose.

The men's eyes went to her wispy black pubic hair and the pink lips that they only partly concealed. Mary's arousal was obvious; her vaginal lips and surrounding hair were wet with her feminine juices...

"Damn, Eddie, look at that cunt. Wet as hell, already. And it's pretty, ain't it? Cunts don't usually strike me as bein' pretty, but this one does. And she's had kids, too... how many, honey?"

Somewhat to her own surprise, Mary spread her legs slightly to improve their view as she answered.

"Just Jessie, Victor's wife. In a way I wish I'd had more..."

The younger man guffawed.

"Well, maybe it ain't too late, honey. Course I'm not sure about granpaw over there, but I might be able to fix you up. It shouldn't be too hard..."

Eddie snorted.

"Listen to the young bastard brag. Hell, he hasn't even got a kid, and he's talking about a man who's got five kids and three grandkids."

He grinned at his companion.

"Results, sonny boy – that's what counts. Not just talk..."

"Oh, damn it – I think all either one of you do is talk. I want to see a little action."

As she spoke one of Mary's hands wandered down to her black pubic triangle and began to caress the swollen lips of her sex...

"She's right."

Bill stared at her moving fingers for a moment, then stood up with his hard penis waving starkly in front of him.

"Come on, Eddie, let's take Mary to bed. She deserves it, and I'm ready too..."

The older man made no reply but stood up and smiled at Mary as he took her unoccupied hand and put it on his erection.

"I'll follow wherever you lead,

sweetheart..."

But the atmosphere changed in some subtle way and suddenly all three were serious about prompt action. The men took Mary's arms and led her to the suite's bedroom while she walked between them with a hand on each hard penis.

Once in the bedroom both men undressed quickly while Mary disposed of her garter belt and stockings. She licked her lips as she looked expectantly at the bed, wondering how they would want her. Any position was satisfactory to her, as long as there was no delay.

And the men seemed equally serious. Eddie took her arm again and led her to the bed. He paused and looked at the younger man.

"Bill, why don't you sit against the headboard. Then Mary can kneel in front of you so she can suck your prick while I fuck her puppy style. Okay?"

"Sounds good to me."

Bill was already on the bed, and he moved somewhat clumsily to the top of it and sat down with his thighs spread. Mary's eyes went automatically to his penis, and she was pleased to see that it had lost none of its hardness...

"Okay, Mary, you next. Get in position so you can get your face in his lap, then get your little ass up in the air. Sometimes I think dogs have the right idea."

He paused as Mary got on the bed and moved up so that she was on her knees facing Bill. She looked into his grinning eyes for a moment, then down at his penis as she again captured it in one hand. But she did not immediately take it in her mouth; she looked over her shoulder to watch the second men climb into position behind her. Mary was on her knees, with her thighs spread and her lush bottom prominently displayed.

Eddie was impressed by the display. On his own knees behind her, he paused long enough to run his hands over the white moons of Mary's bottom. The flesh of her buttocks was both soft and firm, and her position caused them to separate enough to barely reveal the little crevice between them.

The man's eyes travelled down that shadowy indentation, past the dark brown pucker of her anus until they came to rest on the cleft of her vaginal lips. The shiny wetness of her aroused femininity was clearly visible.

"Damn, Mary – your ass is as pretty as most women's faces." He ran a finger down the little path between her buttocks and paused at the anal opening. "You like to take prick up your asshole, baby? I had a woman one time that had rather bugger than fuck. For some reason she could come quicker that way. How about you?"

Mary was still watching him over her shoulder as she quivered from the touch of his finger on her little sensitive rectum's opening.

"I… it's okay, you can fuck me there if you want to. But you'll have to go slow – it usually hurts to begin with."

Eddie's finger pushed slowly into the tight orifice.

"Don't make no difference. If you'd rather take it in your cunt it's okay with me. I'm gonna have a damn good come wherever I fuck you..."

"Hey, baby – remember me?"

Bill put a hand on Mary's chin and gently turned her face around toward him.

"Don't worry about granpaw back there behind you – he'll make out okay. What you want to do is pay some attention to this prick here in front of you. It sure needs some lovin' bad..."

He released her chin as Mary looked down at the penis that she still held in her hand. Then she smiled as she looked up into his face.

"Okay, lover – I'll suck your prick for you."

She turned once more to see the man behind her.

"Go ahead and fuck me, Eddie. But if you want my asshole please get something to put on your prick. I can't take it up my ass dry..."

This requirement seemed to make up the man's mind.

"Hell, I'll just fuck your cunt. We haven't got anything... anyway, your pussy looks too nice and juicy to pass up."

He moved closer to Mary, and she felt his fingers go under her buttocks and dip into the liquid depths of her vagina. But their exploration was brief; he quickly pulled them out of her channel and replaced them with the head of his hard penis.

"Okay, honey, after all the talk let's have some action. Spread your legs a little more, if you can. That's it – good. Now, honey – I'm gonna fuck your cunt good."

Mary was inclined to believe his statement as she felt his penis surge into her waiting channel. She closed her eyes to enjoy the full experience of his entry.

"Mary, baby – you keep ignorin' poor ole Bill. Take my prick and suck hell out of it – or the come out of it, anyway... move, honey, I can't wait any longer."

And Mary did move; as she felt the man behind her penetrate fully and then pull back to begin his strokes she bent her head to Bill's lap and took his penis into her mouth without further delay. And almost at once she felt indications of orgasm; having her body worked on by two men at once was almost more than her aroused nervous system could take.

The man sitting in front of her closed his eyes and leaned back against the headboard as his hands rested lightly on her white shoulders. He relished Mary's technique with the thought that a woman needed more than a simple willingness to take a man's organ in her mouth and suck on it. Mary's action was a work of art; her tongue combined with her soft and warm mouth to caress and pull on every square centimeter of his shaft's surface. Simultaneously one of her hands was around the base as she coordinated a manual pumping motion with the suction of her mouth, the other hand had gone lower to find the wrinkled sac of his testicles so that she could tease and roll the two little mounds of hardness in a way that added to the eroticism of the moment. Bill began to quiver periodically; his orgasm, too, was close.

At the foot of the bed the older man's situation was no less than rewarding. He now drove furiously into Mary's willing vagina with thrusts that barged into her buttocks and shook her whole body. At times he leaned over her back to reach beneath her to grasp the heavy, hanging globes of her breasts. His touch was not gentle; he pressed and rolled the firm flesh harshly even as his fingers found and pulled the hard buds of her nipples.

Mary groaned in passion from this double attack, but little of the sound escaped from her filled mouth. She had already enjoyed two preliminary orgasms, but she had somehow managed to keep them to a relatively low level on the erotic scale as she held her big response in reserve for the men's climax. But her ability to schedule her body's reaction was limited, and the pretty, pale-skinned oriental woman who was now giving her body so enthusiastically to the two men knew that she could not restrain a truly shattering orgasm much longer.

In desperation she pulled her mouth momentarily from Bill's penis.

"I... I'm ready – I'm going to come. You boys get ahead and shoot in me if you can – I can't wait. I want to feel you fill me up with come – both of you. Hurry – oh, please hurry!"

Without waiting for a reply Mary bent again to Bill's lap and quickly recaptured his throbbing penis in her mouth. She immediately sensed that his climax was near, and his hoarse voice confirmed it as his hands tangled roughly in her hair and jammed her mouth farther down on his shaft.

"Take it – suck it. Oh damn, suck my prick, you sweet fuckin' bitch. I'm gonna blow my nuts. Take my come and eat it – swallow it..."

Behind Mary the other man was also speaking, but his words were low and incoherent. But his action gave a clear picture of his feelings; his body jammed violently against Mary's exposed bottom on every stroke. The ferocity of his action threatened to collapse the whole bed...

And then Mary's major climax began. She could not cry out, but her busy mouth redoubled its efforts on Bill's penis as her moans of passion seemed almost to come from the organ in her mouth. And her increased action triggered his release; Bill clinched his teeth together as he felt the first spurt of semen shoot from his penis into Mary's desperate mouth.

"There it is! I'm comin' – comin'! Take it – take my come! Swallow it! Oh damn – damn..."

And only seconds behind the other two, Eddie's orgasm exploded into Mary's vagina. He hunched wildly against her threshing bottom as his motions now timed themselves to the rhythm of his ejaculation...

And then they were all past their peak. Both men continued to hunch into Mary's used body but their tempo tapered off as the after pleasure waned and an almost unbearable sensitivity increased. Mary's feelings lingered longer than the men's, but the last part of her pleasure was diluted by a sudden feeling of degradation. Even as her sensitive body still wallowed in the physical sensations of her orgasm her mind regained partial control. And the thoughts in her mind were not pretty ones... Mary suddenly saw a bleak and sordid picture of herself on her knees before one man who had his penis in her vagina and in front of another man whose semen she could still taste as his softening penis still filled her mouth. And, in the final analysis, she was here for one thing – money. Damn – it was hard to see how she could think of herself as anything but a whore, after this...

She quivered as the man behind her extracted his limp penis and rolled over beside her as he gasped for air with his eyes closed. Mary pulled her face away from Bill's lap and watched his soft organ, glistening with a combination of her saliva and his semen, fall listlessly to his thigh.

Mary felt tired, dirty, and degraded. She wanted a douche, a bath, and, most of all, to leave these two men and this motel as quickly as possible. But this was easier said than done. Bill's hand in her hair reminded her of her position in the scheme of things as she still knelt before him on the bed with her head bowed to try and conceal the tears in her eyes.

And then his voice made it even more positive.

"Nice, Mary, that was real nice. I like the way you suck prick, and looks like Eddie enjoyed your cunt. Tell you what – for the next course I want to try that little asshole of yours. Got me to thinking about it listening to Eddie talk about buggerin' you. Never had a chinky-China girl up the ass. You'll probably have to suck me hard again. Well, there's no big rush; maybe if we wait a little ole Eddie will even be able to get another hard on. You want to go to the bathroom or anything?"

Mary made no reply as she got off the bed and moved icily toward the bathroom. The cheap racial crack was all she needed to plunge her into a mood of hopeless pessimism about her life. As a practicing whore she should have brought a full kit of douche supplies. Well, she'd probably have plenty of opportunities to develop her professional skills...

Mary slammed the bathroom door and splashed water over her face, then looked at herself in the mirror as she gargled some water in an ineffective effort to cleanse her mouth. The ritual was more symbolic than practical...

The night was going to be a long one. When she came back into the room, the men both eyed her up and down, grinning; they seemed to be in a mellow mood, not least because of the whisky highballs they were drinking. Judging from the state of his semi-erect cock, Bill was obviously still keen to pursue his ambition of fucking her in the ass.

Well, at least I'm fairly well acquainted with what's going to go up my bottom, she thought, ruefully.

She stood in front of them, naked and trying to enter into the spirit of the occasion. But it was hard. She still felt dirty, somehow, and now she was to be subjected to yet another invasion of her tender body. Bill came over to her but Eddie made no effort to move from his chair. He smiled at them with approval. She guessed that he was just going to sit this one out and play the voyeur.

Somewhere in the back of her mind, she felt that she should be uncomfortable with him just sitting there watching her while his business partner satisfied his perverse sexual kink. But she didn't. In fact, she found herself admitting she enjoyed the thought of the older man watching them. And that Eddie's hand was gripped tightly around the fully erect length of his cock, slowly jacking it, only added to the excitement that was filling her body. Smiling back, she turned her back to him and leaned over the couch as Bill had directed. With her arms out-stretched to fully support her weight, she spread her legs, opening her body up to the rear attack that would come shortly.

The younger man was behind her now. The fat head of his cock nudged at the upturned curves of her buttocks. She could feel the warm wetness of his preseminal oils smearing their clearness over her skin as his cock jumped and jerked with its excitement.

From the depths of her sexual memory, Mary recalled a deliciously thrilling method that a lover had once used on her to prepare her anus to take his cock. She shivered. The thought of Bill's mouth kissing and licking at her anus and the soft warmth of his tongue probing into the little pucker of her ass was enough to drive her wild. She did her damnedest to relax, knowing that if he used this technique of anal foreplay on her, she would go rigid with excitement.

She trembled as his hands reached out and soothingly roved over the upjutting half-moons of her hind cheeks. He was gentle. His hands tenderly whispered the command to relax and prepare herself for the entry he was going to make into her bowels. She once more, she forced herself to untense, letting the soft caresses of his hands lull her toward the state of relaxedness that was needed.

His gently circling palms drifted between her thighs and pressed against the silken softness of them. She eased her legs further apart. He could see the uptilted mound of her pussy now and the moisture of her desire. He could see the dampened, sparse black pubic hair covering her outer labia like a soft, downy carpet.

His hands slowly and gingerly massaged at the plump knoll for a few seconds, then once again, his finger wiggled into the wet pocket of her cunt, still slick with the older man's sperm. She whimpered with the unexpected invasion of her body, but did not protest, as his finger swirled around, then once again withdrew.

She moaned in mixed disappointment and excitement as she felt his hands grip each of the cushions of her buttocks and spread them. His moist finger dipped into the deep cleft of her ass and stroked at her anus, transferring the juices it had brought from her vagina.

While she would have preferred his mouth and tongue, the finger-to-cunt-to-ass method he used to make her body ready for him was far from a turn-off. First he drilled and pumped his digit into her pussy, whirling around in the abundant juices that readily flowed within her.

Then he returned to her anus, slickening the tiny ringed mouth with a supply of the natural lubricants he had taken from her soaking pussy.

Over and over, he repeated the process. His finger slowly worked its way up into her ass. Then it glided in and out, as he oiled the tight channel with her own juices. She moaned as the probing length of his finger pushed its way in and out of her hot ass. The sensation was fantastic, like an appetizer to what was to come next; a sampler that prepared her for the thickness that was coming.

When his fingers finally left the juice-filled mouth of her sex, she could feel him reach up and grasp the rigid shaft of his cock. Relax! she urged herself, anticipating the newness of Bill's cock she was now so willing to take within her body. Relax! she repeated, as she heard him move closer, readying himself for the attack.

Then he was there, sharply driving the full length of his hard sex into her!

But he wasn't in her ass!

He had plunged his full, throbbing shaft deeply into the vulnerably exposed, upturned slash of her cunt. She groaned. Her ass wiggled in a provocative dance against his groin. Her whole body trembled under the abrupt impact.

Despite the complete surprise of his manoeuvre, she relished the long hardness that packed deeply into her pussy. Perhaps he's changed his mind, she thought in the sudden confusion of the moment, though not really minding. He felt good inside her. And at the moment, that was all that mattered. She had to admit to herself, that Bill and Eddie's earlier activities had left her body aroused. Bill's delicious finger-fucking had only tripled the excitement. Now all she wanted was to be fucked and have the consuming desires of her body released. Immediately, her hips began to work with his pelvis as he pumped himself in and out of her.

Yes, she moaned to herself, yes, this is it. This is good!In and out, he plowed into her cunt, shafting himself in deep, grinding strokes. His crotch slapped into her uptilted ass, making a sharp little popping sound as they collided flesh on flesh. She rocked back and forth, sliding on and off the plunging length of manmeat that impaled her over and over. She rose, climbing higher and higher on the clouds of pleasure. Her whole body focused on the thickness of his sex and the hard length that plowed into the furrow of her pussy.

He rocked her, his hips whipping back and forth. He speared her, his rod of cock pumping in and out. She was close, closer than she could believe, especially since her earlier orgasm had increased her sensitivity. But this stranger, this 'client' to her 'whore', had her going again. Her spread thighs were throbbing at an ever increasing rate. Her body was quaking as waves of heightening pleasure washed through her.

NO!

No! No! No! *Nooooooo!*

The deep-rooted stalk of his manhood had suddenly jerked free from the sheathing channel of her belly with a wet sucking sound. She was empty, hollow, abandoned on the very edge of her release. Her body quaked and screamed in violent protest.

"Oh Bill! God! Oh, my God!"

The complete thickness and hardness of his

prick was suddenly embedded to the hilt in her ass. The shock of the abrupt impalement was almost painful. She knew it would have been, had it not been so quick.

But, instead, she only felt packed. She felt every throbbing inch of his unyielding cock slammed deeply into the tight tunnel of her rectum.

This enormous pole of flesh filled her body. He was a brand of fire shoved firmly into her bowels, burning with a sexual heat that swirled and flamed in a sunburst of lust.

In an involuntary reaction, her muscles clamped with viselike tightness around the column of sex that invaded her. She heard his pleasure-filled moans above her own grunting groans. She pushed and squeezed trying to expell the massive rod that stuffed her so fully. But he remained. His thickness remained firmly implanted in the pushing and squeezing channel of her back. He throbbed and pulsed, jerking with dark and incomprehensible lust.

His hands were back on her buttocks, slowly caressing the creamy smoothness of her pale ass cheeks. The message of his palms penetrated the shock-ridden clouds of her mind. Relax, it said, quelling the violent quivering of her ass muscles. She once again let his hand lull the tenseness of her body. Slowly, but surely, the taut squeezing vise of her anal ring went slack, rippling over the rigid length of his cock. She accustomed herself to him, feeling out his full size and knowing she was quite capable of taking all that he could give her.

Still, he did not move. Instead, he just stood there, his body washed in the exquisite velvet tightness of her ass. His cock was drenched in the fiery heat of her bowels. Her ass squeezed down on him again. This time the violent desperation of her first clutch was gone. Now her tightness came more as a relishing caress. He moaned deeply as his prick jerked and throbbed.

In a slow circling movement, her upturned ass wiggled as she squeezed and relaxed the smooth sheath of her asshole. His groaning rose, echoing a little within the den. She picked up the tempo of her swaying hips, washing the thickness of his rod in a ball-aching flare of exciting friction. Then his hips moved. Outward his big cock came. The walls of her ass tunnel strained out and over the blood-gorged knob of his glans as he pulled from her. The emptiness he left in his wake was five times worse than the sudden wrenching from her pussy.

Further and further, he pulled until only the plump crown of his prick was embedded in the tiny, squeezing mouth of her back passage. She wiggled a little and he groaned.

As she did, his pelvis started inward. Forcing her body to relax, she accepted the ponderous mass of his sex. Inward the unbending pole of his manhood drilled back into her ass. Inch by inch, she accommodated him, as he strained and stretched the round, smooth socket of her rear.

Her body came alive again, trembling with hungry delight as he entered.

Deeper and deeper the throbbing heat of his cock penetrated, rooting itself into the velvet recesses of her rectum. His crotch pressed into her ass cheeks and his hips jerked forward a little, spearing his cock even deeper.

She moaned, clutching at the bigness of his sexual rod. Her ass clamped lovingly around the pulsing circumference that plugged her asshole. Her hips gyrated again, swirling the volcanic heat of her bowels around him.

Then he was pulling free again, slowly, as if unwilling to give up the well-rooted depths he had achieved, but at the same time unable to remain still. She relaxed and let him withdraw, quivering as his movement set off a whole series of blazing sensations.

As he inched his way back into her rectum, she forced her body to remain calm, allowing him to probe back into the seething depths he had set afire with desire. Over and over, he stroked slowly in and out of her, as if he were getting the feel of unfamiliar territory.

Then, as his pace increased, her ass started working on its own. Relaxing, she accepted all of the burning sex brand he could give her. As he withdrew, she squeezed tightly down, delighting in the pleasure-aching moans that she drew from his throat.

Her own hips still circled in their provocative dance, but now they moved up and down, helping him as he fucked her with taunting slowness. It was under the slow-motion pace of his prick that she once more began the rise toward the foothills of pleasure from where his abrupt exit had so rudely wrenched her. Her whole body was alive again. Every nerve was opened to the arousing sensations he sent rocketing through her. In and out, he plowed into the quivering furrow of her ass. She focused her being on the thickness of his fleshy piston, worshipping the filling mass of its size.

Although she could not see him, she thought about Eddie, who sat watching the expert shafting of her body, and wondered if the scene he now viewed was affecting him the way their sexual play had gotten to her? But she knew she really didn't care. All she cared about was the growing hunger of her lust-laden body and the adamantine pole of flesh that moved in and out of her ass in a steady rhythm.

Her greed for cock got the better of her and her hips jerked quickly back and forth. Behind her, Bill got the message and immediately increased the rocking of his pelvis. No longer did he inch his way into her bowels, but glided in a long, smooth stroke, then reversed his motion and slithered outward.

It was good, but she wanted more. Her hips increased the pace once again and he responded. Their bodies met in a spongy sort of cushioned thud, crotch to buttocks. The hairy sac of his testicles slapped at the upturned curves of her hind mounds.

She gyrated and swirled around his ever moving cockshaft. He groaned and slammed into her. She squeezed and sucked at his length, relishing every fat inch of pleasure he fed into her. She rocked back and forth, aiding in the repeated impalement of her body.

His hands gripped into her butt, his fingers digging roughly into the firmness of her ass cheeks. He clung to her, using her buttocks for support. His hips lurched and once more he quickened the tempo of his anal spearing.

Groaning with delight, she accepted him over and over. Her own body met his rhythm. She bucked backwards into him, driving his plunging rod deeper and deeper into the volcanic depths of her ass. Then she jerked away from him, wrenching the pole of sex from her.

Her body quaked under the ever increasing impact of his body. He seared in and out of her and she loved it and wanted more. Which is exactly what he gave her. His crotch slapped loudly into her buttocks now, jarring her and setting the soft, hanging orbs of her tits jiggling back and forth.

Then Bill pulled her her up and towards him so that he fell back onto the bed with her on top. Suddenly she was sitting astride him, facing away from him, but still impaled on his hard flesh pole.

Eddie came over to watch, his hand gently jerking his cock, but Mary was almost unaware of his presence, so absorbed was she by the extraordinarily wonderful sensations in her ass.

She grunted and moaned as the fever of ardent lust grew and blazed outward. She lurched down into him, now riding him, trying to bury the stiff shaft of sex even deeper into her ass. He slammed up into her, pistoning in and out of the tight, clinging tunnel of her rectum.

She wanted to cry out, urging him on harder and deeper, but he pounded upwards, jarring the words from her throat so that only aroused hisses of flaming desire were emitted into the air. She felt it was growing now. Hot and higher it swirled within her. Flaming outwards from her seething asshole, it consumed her loins and set the sensitive button of her clit to aching.

She looked up. Now Eddie was very close to the buggering couple, his eyes glazed with lust as he masturbated openly in front of them. His purple-headed cock looked angry and ready to shoot. Mary's ass rose up and down, swallowing up and sucking at the thick shaft of cock that filled her.

Harder and harder, he speared. Like a jackhammer of flesh, Bill thrust himself up into the burning recesses of her anal tunnel. His balls were lashing with fire, boiling as the need for release grew. He grunted as he slammed and shafted into the sweet tightness of her anal sheath.

Mary's fingers rose to torment her stiff, swollen nipples, then one hand dove down to strum her blood-engorged little bean of a clitoris. She cried out with lust and rose up from sitting to kneeling. She stayed quite still while Bill jackhammered up into her like he had gone crazy, *slap,slap, slap, slap*... her delicate oriental features were screwed up in a mask of lust as she approached her peak of pleasure.

She came first, her whole body erupting. Ecstasy unleashed within her in a wildly flaring nebula. She cried out her satisfaction, as quake after soul-shattering quake of relief and pleasure washed through her body. Her ass contracted and trembled, sucking greedily at the length of his prick.

From behind, she heard him groan and his hips suddenly lurched up for one last time, driving his shaft more deeply into her rectal tube than ever before. The fat crown of his shaft jumped and jerked. Then she felt him tense, she heard him groan, she became aware of the increase in lubrication and the wet warmness, as the juice of his desire spilled into the recesses of her bowels.

Spurt after spurt blasted into her, as his hands gripped her hips and she swiveled and ground her bottom down as if trying to impale herself completely. She could feel every little throb of his release and she loved every tiny quiver of his shaft.

Gratefully locked together, ass to cock, they

groaned and whimpered in the magnificent sensations of their mutual climax. She fell forward and gave a little gasp when a wet trickle of cum escaped as his cock quickly shrunk inside her.

"Mary, look up! Look at me, that's right!"

It was Eddie. Purple in the face, eyes staring, he was close to ejaculating. Mary leaned back, holding her head high, proudly, her beautiful body flushed and shining with the sweat of her exertions.

Eddie gasped, then gave a long, shuddering groan as thick ropes of semen blasted from the tip of his cock to land over her face and hair; Mary felt them drip down and run in sluggish rivulets between the valley of her breasts.

Chapter 4

Mary looked up from the oven as Jessie entered the kitchen in Victor's triplex.

"Good morning, honey."

She glanced at the clock on the wall.

"Just barely, though. Another twenty minutes and it'll be afternoon."

The pretty girl did not seem to be in a cheerful mood.

"Oh, Mom, don't make cracks. I know I

should have been up earlier, but I just lay there, thinking about – everything. I didn't mean to make you fix breakfast – at least not for Victor. What kind of a mood was he in?"

Mary closed the oven door and looked at her daughter. They had hardly seen each other in the two days since Victor and Jessie returned from their honeymoon, and Mary was startled by the girl's drawn appearance.

"Honey, you look like you're completely beat. Of course I guess that's the way you should be after a honeymoon..."

Jessie cut her mother off.

"Mom, please – our honeymoon was... oh well – to put it mildly – pure hell. What is there to eat? I'm not really hungry, but I guess I need something..."

Mary was suddenly concerned about her daughter. For several days now, she had been concerned about her own position in this crazy scheme that she had created, but for the first time she sensed that Jessie had also had problems.

"Honey, sit down at the table and I'll pamper you, just this once. I'll fix anything you want. Eggs... we've got some excellent sausage..."

The young girl shuddered.

"Gee, no, Mom. I couldn't take sausage if my life depended on it. Just some cold cereal and coffee. And some orange juice if there is any. That's all I could possibly eat. I'll fix it if you want me to."

Mary was studying her offspring intently.

"No, I said I'd do it this time."

She paused and looked directly at Jessie as the girl sat with lowered eyes.

"Baby, something's bothering you, and I'm sure it involves Victor. I think we need to talk. I hadn't meant to talk to you about things, at least not just now, but I can see you've got some problems too. So I think we'd better both unload. Did something happen on the honeymoon?"

A half hour later both women were staring into cold coffee cups. The conversation had been frank and enlightening for both mother and daughter. Mary understood, for the first time, the full dimensions of their problem.

She put down the cup she had been toying with.

"Well, I just don't know what to say. The irony of it all, of course, is that I dreamed up the whole damn plan. I thought it was a real clever to give all three of us what we wanted: me, some sort of financial security for the rest of my life; you, the man of your dreams, a rich and successful husband; Victor, as enough pussy to keep him on the straight and narrow of married life – more or less. The trouble was that I just didn't understand Victor at the time."

She paused as she looked at the young girl.

"Jessica, Victor is sick. You realize that, don't you?"

Jessie nodded slowly.

"I... I'm beginning to. I tried not to admit it to myself for a long time. But when he hired that... whore to spend the first night of our honeymoon with us, it was pretty obvious. I didn't know then what he had made you do. Oh gosh, Mom, in a way he must be completely off his rocker. Of course we're partly to blame for ever starting it all – and I'm every bit as much responsible as you are – but at least we thought everything would just be between the three of us; in the family, so to speak. I never dreamed that he would make you let men fuck you or do what he did on the honeymoon. Talk about something seeming unreal – this whole thing is really unreal. Sometimes I just can't believe that it's all happening..."

Mary rose and went once more to the coffee maker on the stove.

"Well, it *is* happening. The one thing I haven't had any trouble with is believing that it's real. God, that night in the motel was real... There's about another cup left. You want it?"

Jessie shook her head.

"No more. I think coffee's about to come out my ears now. Oh, Mom – what do we do? How do I handle this thing?"

Mary looked at her daughter thoughtfully.

"I can't answer that. He's your husband – you'll have to make the decision. I can tell from the way you talk that you're not ready to leave him. Am I right?"

The pretty young wife turned tear-filled

eyes up to her mother.

"No, I guess I'm not. I've thought about it, and I nearly left him several times while we were on the trip. But… oh, gee, I don't know. I must still love him, although I don't really understand why. But Mom – you don't have to take any more of it. He has no right to make you do things like the other night. If you want to pull out of it I don't blame you. Maybe I will too, a little later. But for some reason I just can't do it yet…"

Mary stared unseeingly out the kitchen window as she took a sip of the barely warm coffee. She tried to guess what her daughter's reason was, to empathise, but came up with nothing more than a series of muddled guesses as to the emotional turmoil Jessica was experiencing.

"Honey, get real! If I leave, then we break the 'agreement' and Victor will divorce you, of that I'm pretty sure, so if that's the way you feel, I'll stay with you. Something tells me that any divorce settlement that Victor's lawyers would give you wouldn't be a generous one, either. At least he could hold the threat over your head… no, I'll play it out to the end with you. I started it, after all… And it'll have to go one way or the other, it can't just go on like this. Maybe there's some chance Victor will make a change for the better…"

* * *

"An excellent dinner. Mary, darling, besides your talent with your vagina and your mouth you're an excellent cook. Are you making Jessie help you? I want her to learn to cook as well as you do."

Victor paused and smiled as he got up from the table.

"Of course there are other even more important talents that I want you to help me develop in her. She's still labouring under the naive delusion that the only place a girl should take a man's prick is in her cunt. I have to admit that her cunt is becoming increasingly proficient, but as you know that's only part of the story. I tried to train her a little while we were away, but she didn't respond very well to her 'tutorials'."

He turned to look at her quizzically.

"I suppose you know all about that by now. Well, Mary – what do you think? Will we ever get Jessie to be a fully-fledged woman instead of the little girl she is now?"

Mary tried to keep her feelings out of her voice.

"I don't know how things are going to work out, Victor. Actually, I think Jessie is probably living up to her end of the bargain pretty well. She wasn't supposed to offer a lot of variety, you know, and you've said yourself that she's satisfactory as far as straight sex goes..."

The man laughed.

"'Straight sex'. Oh, Mary, you really kill

me up with your euphemisms. What you mean is plain fucking. Why don't you say what you mean? Do you feel that even those words are too much for your daughter's delicate sensibilities?"

In spite of herself Mary was slightly amused. His point was well taken; everything considered it was a little silly to be so concerned about the vocabulary. On the other hand, his speech was sometimes more vulgar than necessary. Aggressively so.

"...try to educate her, at least. Why don't you tell Jessica about the things we've done, over and above what she considers to be normal. And call things by their real names – don't go clinical on us. That way do you think she'll really ever learn anything?"

Mary's mind had wandered; she had lost the thread of his conversation. His last words had made it sound like he wanted her to give Jessie a lesson in the vulgar, puerile language that he so enjoyed... She hesitated.

"Victor... I'm not sure I understand what you..."

Her son-in-law cut in with a weary voice.

"Oh hell, Mary, you understand, all right. I'm saying that we ought to increase Jessie's sex vocabulary, and at the same time make her appreciate the finer points of sexual intercourse. Hell, it'd be tragic for her to go clear through life without doing anything more than she is now. Explain some of the possibilities to her. After all, proper education is a parental responsibility, isn't it?"

Mentally, Mary shrugged; she saw that Victor was not to be put off. She was under no illusions about his real intent; she was well aware that his main purpose in this respect was to indulge himself in his pastime of listening to lewd language spoken by women. Well, hell – if that was what he wanted...

Mary turned to her daughter.

"Maybe Victor's got a point, darling. The things he likes to do have a place, alright... I guess we've done most of them, and I think we've both enjoyed them..."

Victor's growing impatience was clear.

"Oh, hell, Mary. Spare us the generalities. Tell Jessie, in detail, about some of the things we've done."

Mary choked off her real feelings as she made herself look at the younger girl. Jessie had not finished eating, but she sat across the table with her mind obviously no longer on food as she looked at her husband and mother. She detested the thing that he was making Mary do, and perhaps the larger question was whether she did not now detest her husband, period...

"Well, I'm still waiting, sweet mother-in-law..."

Mary made herself talk.

"Jessie, maybe Victor's right; at least maybe you ought to try some of the things he has in mind. There are a lot of things involved in a complete sexual relationship besides straight intercourse... fucking, of course. I suppose Victor and I have tried the principal ones. I've taken his prick up my asshole, he's buggered me. I'd forgotten how much I enjoy being assfucked. You know that I've sucked his cock and let him come in my mouth. Most men go wild over this, and most of them want you to swallow their jism when they shoot it. But I'll let you in on a little secret – if you suck him right, including when he climaxes, the average man won't care much whether you really swallow it or not. They all say they want you to swallow their sperm, before you suck them, but usually there's a period during their recovery after orgasm when they don't really give a damn about anything. Of course there are exceptions. I've heard of one man who always makes the woman who sucks him spit the come out in her hand and then lick it up again and swallow it. There's probably no way to fool him. But most men aren't like that..."

"Hey, this isn't exactly what I had in mind."

Victor's voice showed some aggravation, but there was also a trace of laughter in it as he realized what Mary was doing.

"Told you to educate Jessie, but not in the art of fooling her partner. Now, suppose you get back on course here, and finish telling her about what we do. No, hell, wait..."

Victor paused and seemed to think, then

reach a decision.

"Hell, never mind the explanations. There's one thing that Jessie *did* agree to, through some quirk of fate. She did accept the idea of making love with you, and I think it's time that we had a little female session..."

Both women drew a sharp breath and looked at each other. What Victor said was true, and represented an anomaly in Jessie's attitude that Mary had never understood.

And Jessie, too, was unsure why she had agreed to this particular act, which was one that would be considered particularly perverted by most conventional standards. Maybe it was that she had just never believed that her husband would actually ask such a thing.

"Well, I don't hear any comment. I'd think that two pretty females like you would be anxious to get at each other's cunt. I sure as hell enjoy both of your cunts, so I'm sure you will too."

Mary finally turned a serious face toward the man.

"Victor, I'm not sure this is the time. I know Jessie agreed to it, but I think some time later on when things are..."

"Later on, hell. I'm ready for it right now, and there's no reason for her not to be, too."

Victor looked directly at his downcast wife.

"Jess, baby, it's time to drop this prima donna complex that you've got. I'm gonna keep my bargain; I'm not gonna make you do anything that I agreed not to. But that's exactly the point – you did agree to love making with your mother. So there shouldn't be any problems – right?"

Mary watched her daughter struggle with herself. She knew that Jessie was making a quick review of the whole situation, and she also knew that it was really a waste of time – she was not ready yet to leave her husband, and this meant that she would have to comply with his wishes, perverted as they were... And then Mary's mental focus changed as she considered, for the first time, the idea of sex with her daughter. Thoroughly heterosexual, Mary had nevertheless enjoyed the half dozen encounters with her own sex that she had, for one reason or another, experienced over the years. And certainly Jessie was more attractive as a female than any of the others had been. But Jessie was her *daughter*, and it would be *incest*, damn it!

Somewhat similar thoughts were in Jessie's mind. She had had no previous lesbian experience, but she had heard such things discussed in detail by some of her friends. Her feelings about such an act with her mother were mixed; she loved her beautiful and sensual mother more than any other female, and from that point of view Jessie knew that she had rather make love to Mary than to any other woman. But Mary was her mother, and while they often kissed and hugged and petted one another, there was never anything remotely sexual about their physical affection; what Victor was suggesting added the extra dimension of perversion that the man seemed to find so interesting. Well, hell... the central fact was that she had no choice, unless she was prepared for a major crisis and probably the end of her marriage...

"Well, you two seem to be lost in thought."

Victor's voice had a touch of sarcasm.

"I'd think that you'd both be tickled to death. I can't think of two more suckable cunts than you have."

He turned to his wife.

"Tell me, honey, in detail – how do you feel about sucking your mother's pussy? After all, it can't be an entirely new experience – you've been there before."

Victor's smile was sardonic as he searched for Jessie's reaction to his crude joke.

Jessie could not make herself look at her husband.

"Oh, Victor – do I... I mean, do we really have to do it? Why would you want us to... you know neither of us want to do such a thing. Please – can't we just forget it?"

Her husband gave a mirthless little laugh.

"Forget it? Hell no, we can't forget it. It's part of the arrangement that I've been looking forward to ever since Mary proposed this little deal. I've just been waiting for the right time, and I've decided that this is the right time."

He paused as he stared at his distraught wife.

"Jessica – look at me. Look at me, damn it.

That's better. Now – are you going to carry out your end of the arrangement? Are you going to suck your mother's pretty oriental cunt, and let her suck yours? I want a straight yes or no. And you'd better consider all the consequences before you answer no..."

Jessie knew instinctively that hesitation on her part would only increase her husband's perverted sense of power. She forced herself to turn moist eyes up to his intent face.

"Alright, if you insist. I'll do it."

The man seemed both pleased and disappointed by her answer.

"Oh, damn it – you'll do what? Jessie, you're at least going to learn the language of sex. I've told you that before. Now – tell me in detail what you're going to do. Do you understand me? In detail..."

With a lack of hesitation that surprised all of them, herself perhaps most of all, Jessie faced her husband squarely.

"Alright, Victor. I'll suck mom's cunt, if that's what you want to see. And lick her asshole. And suck her tits, and love her all over. If she wants to do the same thing to me, I'll let her."

Jessie shifted her gaze to the lovely woman who was her mother as she continued.

"Mom, I don't really mind, or at least I mean that I'd rather do it with you than anyone as long as it has to be done. I don't know whether you can come from having me suck you or not, but if you can I want you to. I... I don't really know how to do it, but I'll do the best I can. You'll have to tell me if I do anything wrong..."

Mary found herself genuinely touched by the obvious affection that Jessie showed. She suddenly found the total prospect less appalling than it had been. Jessie was a lovely girl, and, after all, they did adore each other... suddenly the taboo, but piquant, thought popped into her head: what would it really be like to make love to your own child? She realised that, the way things were going, she would very soon find out.

"Well, that's all very sweet. Sounds like you about half like the idea, Jessie,"

Victor turned to Mary.

"What about you, Mom? You like the idea of having Jessie suck your cunt?"

Mary turned a level gaze on the man.

"If you want the truth, it doesn't sound so bad right now. Neither one of us have ever thought of such a thing before, but since you're forcing it on us I'll admit that I'm glad it's with Jessie. I love her, and she is sexy, and if there's any perversion involved, then you will have to take the blame for that..."

For an instant Mary thought that she had said too much, but her son-in-law seemed to take her remarks in good humour.

"Your comments are duly noted and entered in the record. I guess you're about right at that, Mary. The only trouble with that theory is that I don't recognize any such thing as perversion.

That word has no meaning, as far as I'm concerned. But, what the hell – we've got too many words and not enough action. I think it's time to adjourn to the living room – or better yet, the bedroom. Since we're being frank, I'll have to admit that the prospect has got my prick hard already."

Victor pushed his chair back from the table and stood up. The eyes of both women went automatically to his crotch where a familiar bulge showed the truth of his statement.

He grinned as he held out his hands to the two women and led them toward the bedroom. "... go on, Jessie. There's plenty of room for your hand, too. Mary won't mind sharing it with you. After all, it is your husband's prick..."

Victor chuckled as he stretched luxuriously. The odd threesome, all nude, lay side by side on the oversize bed in the master bedroom. Victor was between the two females, and he had started the proceedings by having Mary caress his hard penis while Jessie watched. He was now ready for his wife to join in the action.

"Go on, sweets, you've played with my prick before. Your mother doesn't want to hog it all."

He glanced toward Mary.

"Tell you what, Mom – you concentrate on my balls while your bashful little daughter handles my prick. We have to give her something to do, don't we?"

Mary made no answer as she moved her hand off the hard shaft and down beneath it to find the wrinkled sac with which she was already familiar. In spite of herself she felt the old familiar stirrings in her loins... Victor was a bastard, but he did have a talent for creating erotic scenes. There was no way that she could remain unaroused through one of his sessions... And that was probably a good thing, because they would be doubly hard to take if her body failed to respond.

Jess watched her mother fondle Victor's testicles, then brought her own hand to the thick, eight-inch column of his penis. She grasped it and began to squeeze it in an effort to test its firmness. The skin was soft, but the blood gorged muscle beneath the skin was hard and ready. As almost always, it seemed...

Victor lay for a minute with his eyes closed as he delighted in the touches of the two lovely females. The thought struck him that the plan initiated by his beautiful mother-in-law had much to recommend it.

Then he opened his eyes and looked at the women. He brought his hands up and found the firm flesh of Jessie's pert breasts, then transferred his attention to Mary's heavy, hanging globes.

"Well, I can't complain about your tits – either of you. I guess I'm especially lucky where you're concerned, Mary – not many men have a mother-in-law with boobies like yours... or a cunt like yours, for that matter. Of course I guess I've had your mouth and asshole more than your cunt, haven't I? I suppose I've saved most of my straight fucking for my straight little wife... Mary, baby – suck my balls a little. Take them in your mouth one at a time. Or both at once, if you can."

He turned to the younger girl.

"Watch your mother carefully, Jessie. You've got to learn some way... you can keep jacking my prick while she sucks my nuts..."

Mary sighed silently. He always came up with a few extra touches that added to the degradation that seemed to be so important to him. Mary suddenly wondered whether Victor was capable of plain, routine, conventional sex... her experiences with him gave no indication that he was. Always there were those specialized requirements to stimulate him... of course, this was probably to be expected in view of her arrangement with him. The gist of it, after all, was that she was to provide such erotic extras. And apparently he did have normal sex with Jessie, although there was that episode with the whore on their wedding night.

"Mary, dear mother-in-law... I wonder if I could ask for your attention?"

Victor's impatient voice snapped Mary's mind back to the present.

"I don't know what you're daydreaming about – possibly a bigger prick than mine – but since my prick and balls are the ones that concern you at the moment I wonder if you'd concentrate your talent on them. On my balls, for the time being..."

Mary made no reply as she squeezed his testicles in her soft hand. Her touch was gentle, and she restrained an impulse to give them a yank that would put him out of sexual commission for this night, and perhaps longer. But she resisted the urge; as pleasant as the prospect might be, it could only create more problems than it would solve. Her best bet, until Jessie had a change of heart, was to humour him and perform her function without apparent hesitation.

Mary forced herself to smile.

"Alright, Victor. I'd like to take your balls in my mouth. I wonder if they would taste as good individually as the come from them does? I've tasted quite a bit of your come, you know, your thick, *creamy* come."

She turned toward Jessie and, sure that Victor could not see her face, winked.

"Honey, you ought to learn to suck your husband's prick so that he shoots his stuff in your mouth and you can sample his jism. It's delicious..."

Both women felt the man's body respond to Mary's lewd words. His already hard penis throbbed in Jessie's little hand, and Mary thought that she detected an involuntary twitch in his testicles.

And Victor, too, was aware of a sudden increase in his arousal.

"Mary... wait – don't suck my nuts. Afraid

I'll shoot if Jessie keeps playing with my prick. I want both of you to take your hands off me and get in position for a sixty-nine. I'm gonna jack off while I watch you suck each other. Come on – hurry up. We'll do other things later. Right now I want to see both of you eat pussy. Come on – move."

Mary stared at him with the thought that he was pushing Jessie too fast. But, maybe not... if he demanded mutual oral love maybe it was just as well to break her in this way. Maybe it was foolish to worry about degrees of perversion...

"Let's see..."

Victor paused as he looked at mother and daughter and then at the bed.

"Mary, I think the best deal would be for you to stretch out on your back and let Jessie get on top of you."

He turned to his pretty young wife.

"You understand the position, don't you? You straddle Mary facing her feet so that your cunt is over her face. Then when you bend-down on her she spreads her legs so that her pussy is right under your mouth. Got the picture?"

Jessie's voice was cold.

"I've got the picture. I know what a sixty-nine is; it's just that I've never understood why anybody wants to do it. Especially two women..."

Her husband smiled in an unhumorous way.

"That's your problem. And that's why I'm having your mother try to teach you what the score is. Now – let's have a little less talk and a little more action. If you suck Mary's cunt right your mouth will be too busy to talk. Come on – let's go. Mary darling, on your back…"

Mary found herself ready to proceed, and as Jessie and Victor moved to kneeling positions on the edge of the huge bed she lay down in its centre. She stretched momentarily to loosen the muscles that had become a little cramped in her previous position, then straightened out and looked over at the two naked people on the side of the bed as she spread her thighs and brought her knees up slightly with her feet resting flat on the bed. In an almost unconscious gesture she ran one hand down to her loins and brought her fingers into her sparse, silky pubic hair, hair that she knew was less curly than her daughter's thicker, more typically occidental bush. Her fingers went on to the slick inner lips of her sex as she turned to look at Jessie.

"Alright, honey… come over to me. But not over my face, like he said, that's too high. Put your knees about even with my tits – then when you bend down your pussy will be over my face. Come on, darling – I don't mind sucking your sweet little… cunt."

Mary held out one hand to her nervous daughter as her other hand continued to pet her own femininity. She was no longer repulsed by what she was about to do – on the contrary, she was beginning to look forward to the relief that the beautiful girl could provide. Mary's aroused libido required relief of some sort... and, since they had to do it, well...

Jessie, too, faced the prospect of lesbian lovemaking with her mother with much less apprehension than she had expected. She also took refuge in the fact that the act was being forced on them. And, since it was, she was glad that her partner was to be the elegant mother whom she had always loved so much... and who was about the sexiest female she had ever known.

In a partial daze, Jessie moved somewhat ungracefully on her knees toward her waiting mother. Her eyes searched Mary's for reassurance, then went down to the lovely woman's crotch. Jessie felt a strange combination of reluctance and exultation as she looked at her mother's pudenda. She had seen it before, and even under sensual conditions since the beginning of this odd three-way sexual pact, but never as an immediate prelude to actual incestuous, lesbian sex. And yet that thought seemed of small consequence; her gaze now was a more practical one, the speculative one of a sex partner.

Jessie trembled as she felt Mary's hand rest lightly on her buttock as she kneeled, motionless, by her prone mother.

"Jessie, baby... turn this way so I can see your cunny. I've never seen it... I mean, like this. Do you like my cunt? It sounds trite, but it is where you came from..."

Mary listened to her own words almost as though she were another person as she tried to probe her own mind and feelings. She could tell herself that she talked like this to her daughter for Victor's benefit, as a part of the overall charade that had been forced on both of them. And that was at least partly true – but was it the whole truth? Was it also true that she actually was drawn to the lush and appealing body of her own beautiful girl?

Jessie's mind was in a more or less parallel turmoil, but she lacked her mother's capacity for introspection under such unusual circumstances. She knew only that the perverted circumstances of her present life had forced changes in outlook on her – things and acts that would have been repulsive to her a few weeks ago could now be examined for possible merit... The girl's anguished mind was actually unaware of most of the background thoughts running through it as, like the superb computer that the human brain is, it integrated the whole situation and presented her senses with an overall result that, in effect, urged her to explore this opportunity with the desirable female who lay before her...

"Hey, you two – you're pretty like that, just lookin' at each other, but you'll have a hell of a lot more effect on my prick when you suck each other's cunt. For chrissakes, it's not like you were strangers..."

Victor's impatient voice cut in on the confused but necessary mental process of both women. But it prodded those processes with a reminder that they actually had little choice in the matter...

And finally both mother and daughter accepted that fact with a sense of subconscious relief and permitted themselves to slip into a realm of pure erotic sensuality. Mary's caress on Jessie's buttock became more insistent; after a moment she raised herself on one elbow so that she could caress Jessie's nearest breast with her free hand.

"Jessie... Jessie, baby..."

Mary's voice was low as she leaned forward enough to bring her face to the smooth outer surface of Jessie's enticingly perky breast. Mary's cheek rubbed the velvet flesh for a moment, then her eager mouth moved around to capture the rubbery little nipple between her lips.

Jessie's eyes closed as she felt her mother suck her breast. The feeling was at once gentle and intense; she felt the arousal that lips on her sensitive nipple always produced and the sensation was this time magnified by the circumstances, by the fact that it was her own mother's mouth on her breast...

"Mom... oh gee. Mom, I... God!"

Still on the edge of the huge bed, Victor grasped his own penis as he watched the developing tableau with wide eyes. The scene before him was an even more powerful stimulant than he had expected it to be, and it occurred to him that he might not be able to contain his passion as long as he might want too... He had better have them get to the main course of this erotic meal.

"Jessie... go on and get over her – properly. Hurry up. I want you in the sixty-nine position. I want to see you suck cunts. Go on, Jessie... move."

The words and their own needs made the women react. With a final pull on Jessie's erect nipple Mary released her breast and smiled for a moment up into her eyes.

"I want you, too, darling. Are you ready? I want to suck your little cunt. It's not for him, it's for us. Are you ready, baby?"

The young daughter and wife was ready.

"Mom, yes – yes. I want it, too. I want you to suck my pussy, and I... want to suck yours. You'll have to show me – tell me. Mom, I want to do it, I really do!"

The two exquisite females moved without further urging from their male spectator. Mary lay back so that she was once more flat on the bed with her thighs spread and raised. Jessie forced herself to abandon the visual pleasures of Mary's femininity momentarily while she moved into position over the prone woman. She faced Mary's feet and swung one lovely leg across the older woman's chest so that she straddled Mary's bosom. The position of Jessie's legs brought her crotch into full view and spread her soft white buttocks enough to make the crevice between them and her dainty, puckered anus clearly visible to the aroused woman beneath her. Mary responded by bringing both hands up to toy with her daughter's fully exposed and vulnerable vagina. Her fingers traced little patterns along Jessie's neat labia as her eyes continued to feast upon the delicious array of feminine charms.

And Jess was also busy. Supporting herself somewhat awkwardly on one arm, she used the other hand to reciprocate her mother's intimate caress. Her fingers played in the soft black strands of Mary's pubic mound then caressed the warm, wet lips of her vagina. Jessie was enthralled; she had entered the world from the enticing channel beneath her. Suddenly it seemed only proper that she love that channel, too.

With a little moan Jessie closed her eyes and dropped to her mother's body. Her face found the delicate filaments of her mother's bush, so soft and downy against her cheek, and then her luscious lips found the soft, leaking lips of Mary's sex. Instinct guided the aroused young girl; she needed no instruction from either Mary or Victor. Her nose burrowed between the large, succulent lips to spread them so that her pink tongue could find, and sample, the juices that now flowed so copiously from her mother's vaginal tunnel. With sensitive, probing fingers, she parted her mother's inner lips and pulled them back to reveal Mary's sizeable, swollen clitoris.

The sudden attack surprised Mary in its intensity and proficiency. She twitched and rolled gently on the bed as her over-wrought senses reacted to Jessie's inexperienced but highly effective lesbian lovemaking. And then Mary's instinct made her join the sweet erotic battle; her hands went to Jessie's buttocks and pulled the girl's threshing loins down onto her face. Mary found her face covered by Jessie's own dark pubic curls and then her mouth found its delightful target. With somewhat less finesse than she might have used under more relaxed circumstances Mary began a licking, sucking tribute to her daughter's lovely cunt, her tongue wetly parting the neat labial groove until it reached the small but pronounced clitoral hood, where it found the little nub of her daughter's seat of extreme pleasure. Here her tongue flicked and fluttered, licked and lapped until she felt the girl's entire frame start to shudder with delight. Her face, hidden beneath the girl's twisting loins, was quickly soaked with the sweet nectar of Jessie's response.

And the third person in the room was no less affected by the sensual scene than the participants themselves. In an unaccustomed role of spectator, Victor could initially depend only on the sterile action of his own hand on his penis to supplement his visual stimulation.

"Damn, you two must love to eat pussy..."

His words, low, indistinct and slurred by lust, went unheard by the two females as they continued their expressions of love and sex.

But the man was not long to be denied. Still on his knees he waddled clumsily toward the center of the bed.

"Mary... baby, give me one hand. Take my prick and jack it while you suck Jessie's pussy. Here... here, dammit – take my prick."

Victor's hands forced one of Mary's away from Jessie's crotch and brought it to his straining organ. Mary's white fingers closed around it and instinctively began to pull and rub it in a stroking motion. One of Victor's hands covered hers as he set the tempo of her strokes. Then it left his own pubic area and moved to Jessie's upturned buttocks as they pitched and rolled above Mary's working mouth...

Mary had not moved her head to look at Victor; instinct and his hand had made clear his desires. And she had no real objection to this addition to her sexual act; it felt good to have a male connection as she continued to make lesbian love to her daughter.

Jessica Jordan was so immersed in this new experience that she was unaware of Victor's approach and his limited participation. Her world was now centered in the wet flesh of her mother's vagina, and Victor's fingers on and between her buttocks were scarcely noticeable. But she did notice it when one of his fingers invaded her rectum, just above Mary's active tongue. Jess felt yet another explosion of passion; her orgasm was near and she knew that it would be a devastating one...

But, strangely, the least involved person reached culmination first. Victor dug his finger deeper into his wife's rectum as he closed his eyes and threw his head back.

"God... I'm comin'! Jack me – shit, Mary, jack my prick! Make it spurt... oh, damn – I'm comin'! Here it is – take my come! Ohhh *fuck*..."

The man's orgasm was an intense one despite his minor part in the proceeding. His thick white sperm squirted from the organ in Mary's hand in an arc that carried it splattering half-way up Jessie's back and over her buttocks. But Victor did not see it; his eyes were shut as he trembled and shook from the effects of Mary's tight grasp. She pumped his penis, now in a literal sense, as the semen continued to shoot forth, now dribbling slowly down the valley of her buttocks and over her wrinkled pink anus until it reached the hairy split of her her already dripping cunt, to trickle steadily into her mother's open, hungry mouth.

But the older woman was hardly aware of this addition to her daughter's juicy outpouring as all of her senses focused on her own orgasm and that of her Jessie. Her last semi-rational thought before waves of pure passionate fulfillment washed out every other mental awareness was that Jessie, too, was in the throes of climax. Mary sensed it from the condition of her daughter's vagina, and she was intimately aware of that condition as her tongue attacked the girl's sperm-drenched sex with renewed passion.

Neither woman was able to express her ecstasy verbally, but each sensed the other's reaction as they continued to love each other in the most sensual way that females can.

Chapter 5

"... do the best I can. But Victor, damn it, you're going too far too fast. If you really want Jessie to respond, ease up for a while. Besides, this will break your agreement with her."

Mary closed her eyes in disgust as she listened to her son-in-law's rationalizations. It was increasingly clear to her that Victor's perverted desires were changing for the worse. The man might actually be flipping.

She changed the phone to her other ear.

"Alright, I said I'd try. But I think you're pushing too hard. If you'd let up a little and let Jessie have a little time to adjust... alright, damn it, I'll do what I can."

Mary was seething as she hung up the phone. The bastard was going too far... She looked at the clock on her dresser and saw that Jessie would be home in a half hour. Filled with dread of the coming evening, Mary rose slowly and walked toward her bathroom. A warm bath might help a little...

But nothing could make the evening ahead much easier. It would be hard even to tell Jessie about it.

Mary looked bleakly around the well-appointed kitchen. The last thing she felt like doing was preparing a meal, and yet some sort of domestic activity might help keep her mind off the whole mess. But she knew that it could not really help; nothing could keep the terrible situation that she and Jessie were in out of her consciousness. She had been able to think of nothing else for the last week, and things were becoming steadily worse.

"Hi, Mom – am I late? I intended to fix dinner tonight... Mom, you look depressed. Anything wrong?"

The woman turned to face her daughter, her large almond eyes softening with affection.

"You surprised me, baby. I didn't hear you come in. You look good."

Jessie studied her mother intently. They were too close to each other to effectively hide their feelings, and, though neither had spoken of it, their sense of closeness had intensified since their night of enforced lovemaking. Each had both feared and hoped that they might have to make love again.

Jessie hesitated.

"Mom... something's wrong. I can tell. You

better level with me." A sudden thought crossed her mind. "Has... has Victor been home this afternoon?"

Mary smiled, a little grimly. "No, nothing like that. Nothing wrong with me." Suddenly she realized the futility of hiding anything from Jessie. She might as well be told now.

"I did talk to Victor. I... he called, mostly about his plans for tonight, I guess." She paused and looked at Jessie's intense face. "It seems that he's dreamed up something new for us. All of us, I guess."

Mary saw a shadow flick across Jessie's pretty face.

"What are you trying to say, Mom? Do you mean Victor's got a new sex caper of some kind?"

Mary looked away from her daughter.

"Yes. And it's pretty far out. Seems he's bringing home some new equipment for tonight." She turned back to Jessie.

"He's got some dildos, and he's... well, he talks about renting one dog – a trained dog – to join our happy little home for the evening."

Jessie seemed much less shocked than Mary had anticipated.

"Dildos? You mean – for us to use on ourselves? To fuck ourselves with? Well, I don't like it, but I suppose it's one of his milder notions."

She paused, and seemed to be thinking.

"What about the dog? What does he want

with him...? Oh! *Mom* – you don't mean."

Mary nodded.

"Exactly. That'll be a new one for me, too. I've heard of it, but I've never seen it."

Now Jessie was visibly shocked.

"Mom – you mean... you mean he intends for the dog to... to fuck us? Oh, God – surely not!"

Mary's voice was tired.

"I'm sure God has nothing to do with this or with anything else that goes on in that perverted mind of his. Jessie, honey – Victor's mind is perverted. I don't like to say that about your husband, and anyway I guess it sounds funny coming from me, since, as I keep reminding myself, I dreamed up this whole nightmare in the first place. But that's the point – he's gone beyond what I proposed, and he's going farther beyond it all the time. Jessie – Victor is sick, and it won't help anything to refuse to recognize it. What he's talking about for tonight clearly breaks his agreement with you, and he admits it – he doesn't seem to care. Baby, I'm not trying to push you; after all it's your marriage. But you better take a long, hard look at things. The way I see it the whole mess is going from bad to worse and going fast."

Jessie listened to her mother like a little girl being lectured about her playmates.

"Mom, please... let up on me. I... you're probably pretty close to the truth, but what can I do? Besides leave him, I mean. Maybe

I ought to leave him, but... well, I'm just not ready to do that yet. It may come to that, but I want to give it every chance to work out. I... I keep thinking that he'll begin to change in the other direction. Oh, Mom – maybe I'm a fool, but remember I did love him, and I guess it's not all dead yet. Give me a little more time to work with him."

Mary made no reply as she stared at her daughter's lovely but distressed face. She knew that it was useless to argue with Jessie at this stage; she simply was not yet ready to recognize the obvious. Well, in that sense maybe the evening ahead would serve a useful purpose – it might make Jessie finally see Victor as he really is.

* * *

"How do you like them, darling? This is a pretty expensive set. You notice that you have an assortment of sizes and that some of them have an attachment for this belt arrangement so they can be worn by one woman to allow her to fuck another woman. What do you think of them?"

Jessie gazed at the collection of dildos with a kind of morbid fascination. In an expensive leatherette-covered and felt-lined box, the half-dozen imitation male organs were clearly fine examples of the dildo maker's art. About half seemed to be made of a fairly soft plastic and the rest of a harder rubber.

Jessie looked up from the box into the eyes of her husband. She saw in his eyes hints of vague, indefinable things that had been there before. Jessie knew that her mother's feeling that Victor was undergoing fundamental changes was at least partly right, but she refused to admit that the situation was beyond salvage. It was up to her to try to save their marriage, even if it meant submitting to things that were beyond the scope of their agreement.

"Honey, you're a thousand miles away. I asked you how you liked your dildos. They are yours; they're a present from your loving husband. I'm sure you won't be selfish with them; I know you'll share them with your mother."

Jessie tried to control the revulsion she felt as she looked down into the box again. Damn – why would a woman want to use something like that on herself?

"How about you, Mary? Do you like Jessie's little toys? I'm sure she'll let you use some of them."

Victor paused.

"Come to think of it, we'll use them a little right now. Just as a starter, both of you stand over here and pull your skirts up. Come on – over here in front of the couch. Right here – facing each other. A little closer together, but not too close. Okay. Now – pull your skirts up and slip your panties off. Come on, move when I tell you to do something. Get those skirts up and your panties off. I want to see your cunts."

The two women faced each other as they self-consciously began to comply with his orders. Jessie could not bring herself to look into her mother's eyes; besides her natural embarrassment she also felt a sense of guilt, a certain responsibility for the situation because she had refused to follow Mary's advice. And the evening was probably going to be a rough one.

"Good. Good. It's always good to see cunts as pretty as these no matter how many times you've seen them before."

Victor's eyes traveled from Mary's delicate, sparse bush to Jessie's somewhat thicker but equally enticing display of curls as both women stepped out of their panties.

After a moment he again picked up the box of dildos.

"Alright, girls, for a starter I want you to each pick a dildo and use it on yourself a little. See how it feels. I know you've both fucked yourself with things before, but you'll find these much better than anything except a real prick. Mary, you may have used a dildo before. Have you?"

Mary tried to keep her feelings out of her voice as she replied.

"No, Victor, I haven't. I've never had one, and I've never needed one."

His reply was a hollow laugh.

"Oh, come off it. Any woman can find use for a dildo; no one man can fuck her as much as she wants unless she's undersexed. And I'm pretty sure you've never had that problem. Well, hell – let's have a little less talk and a little more action. I want to see a couple of these up your cunts."

He held the box between the partially nude women as they held their skirts above their hips. Both Mary and Jessie stared down at the objects with a fascination they could not control.

"Well, go on – both of you pick one and we'll give them a try. This is a little one sided – all I'll get to do is watch. But that's me – unselfish old Victor. Go on – pick one out."

Both women finally did make a selection. Each took a medium sized example and slowly removed it from the box.

"Good. Those look like they ought to do the job. Well, you know what that job is. Spread your legs so you can get them in your cunts. You'll probably have to lick them to wet them unless your pussies are already wet enough. Be your own judge of that. Well – come on. Don't just stand there and look at them."

Mary moved first. She raised the plastic organ to her lips and tentatively protruded her pink tongue to moisten it. The action produced an odd feeling – she felt at once a little foolish, somewhat embarrassed, and undeniably aroused.

The sensation that resulted from her tonguing of the object was also strange. She had no illusions about its genuineness; only in the most indirect fashion did it resemble actual oral love to a male penis. And yet there was a definite sensuality involved; imitation or not, the fact remained that she intended to put the thing in her vagina and produce an orgasm through its use... and in front of her daughter and son-in-law.

"Come on, Mary – let's see it in your lovely Chinese pussy. Spread your legs a little more and kind of bend your knees if you need to. There – that makes your cunt lips spread a little. Now, take one hand and hold the lips apart while you put it in."

Mary felt a flash of anger.

"Damn it, Victor, you don't have to tell a woman how to jack herself off. I know what to do without your instructions."

But his sudden smile made Mary realize that her protest was self-defeating. Any sign of resistance only increased the man's pleasure. And so Mary came to the conclusion that she had reached so many times before – her best course was to cooperate fully and get the whole episode over with a minimum of friction.

She made herself smile at him as she reached between her legs and spread the lips with the fingers of one hand. Without further hesitation she changed her grip on the plastic, flesh colored dildo and brought the head of it to the lips of her femininity.

"Oh, gosh."

The soft exclamation came from Jessie and made Mary look once more at the pretty girl who stood with her own legs spread in an almost mirror image of her mother's lewd position. Jessie's eyes were locked on the organ that was slowly working its way into the warm depths of Mary's body.

"Feel good, Mary? Feel like a real prick up your cunt? Tell us about it, honey, and do it in detail."

The beautiful Chinese woman standing in the undignified but sensual pose with her legs spread and an artificial penis almost fully into her vagina made herself continue to smile as she looked back at the man who was responsible for this whole ridiculous but erotic scene.

"Yes, it feels good, Victor. Partly because I'm all worked up, I guess. Oh, it doesn't actually feel like a real prick, but it seems to have kind of a special feeling all its own. And the feeling is pretty similar to being fucked. I guess if you were in bed by yourself with the light out it would be pretty easy to imagine that somebody was fucking you."

Mary's words were merely what she thought that Victor wanted to hear, but the dildo did produce a reaction in her aroused body. She gradually worked it into herself to full depth and then left it motionless as her vagina acclimated to the strange but undeniably welcome stranger.

And then Victor turned to his pretty young wife.

"Jessie, darling, what are you waiting for? I want to see your dildo go up your cunt, too. You may need it more than Mary does; when I'm away you can't fuck with anybody else like she can if she wants to. Unless I tell you you can, that is. And by the way I've got something in mind along that line that you ought to really like, at least after you get used to it. But we'll go into that later – right now I just want to see you fuck yourself. Go on, honey – get it in your cunt, just like your mother did."

Like her mother, Jessie accepted the notion that, for the present, compliance was the best policy. And she also knew a certain curiosity and even need – her libido was aroused, and the thing in her hand offered the only immediate means of relief… Jessie closed her eyes as she reached beneath herself and spread the lips of her vulva, then brought the head of the dildo between them. She had not moistened the shaft, as Mary had done, but her vagina was now so wet that it seemed unnecessary.

And then without further urging the distraught young wife made the penetration and plunged the imitation organ to the full depth of her vagina. Unlike her mother, Jessie did not pause to delight in the feeling of full penetration. She immediately drew the dildo almost out of herself, then, with a little moan, plunged it back in as she set a tempo and began to stroke herself… Her eyes were closed and she seemed to have forgotten the other people in the room as she moaned softly and let a little trickle of saliva escape from the corner of her slightly open mouth. Her free hand went to her bosom and began to fondle one breast through her clothes.

Mary watched her daughter in shocked surprise. She had not expected Jessie to react in this uninhibited fashion, although she realized that it was the best way to handle the situation. Mary continued to hold her own dildo motionless as she watched Jessie's increasingly frenzied action.

"Okay, Mary, get with it. Want you two to come at the same time if you can. Damn, looks like Jessie has more natural talent with a dildo than you have."

Mary barely heard Victor's words, but she did begin to move the shaft in her own body. Her eyes were on the movements of Jessie's hand, and unconsciously she began to time her own thrusts to those of her daughter.

The man was also engaged in auto-eroticism. His action was somewhat more conventional as his hand pumped his hard penis. Victor's organ was a large one, but it was not quite as big as the two replicas now in the vaginas of his wife and her mother.

And then Victor's motion on his penis stopped as he looked at the two working females. "Hold it – hold up a minute. I've changed my mind – I don't want you to come yet. Stop, damn it – you hear me?"

His words did finally penetrate the lust saturated minds of Mary and Jessie. Mary responded first, but reluctantly and only partially; she stopped the major motion of the hand that held the dildo but continued a subtle and almost undetectable rotary motion of the shaft in her vagina.

Victor looked at his wife, displeased by her failure to follow his instructions. "Damn it, I said stop, Jessie. Quit fucking your damn cunt. Open your eyes and look at me, damn you. And hold that God damn thing still in your cunt."

The man's growing anger finally cut through the sexual fog that had surrounded Jessie. Disappointed, she nevertheless, stilled her hand and opened her eyes to look at her husband. Husband... damn, could she really have married this man? Could she possibly still love him?

"Okay, that's a little better. You pay attention when I say something, Jessie. Now – I've got an idea for a little refinement or two. First, I want both of you to take your dildos out of your cunts and hold them up in front of you. Now that should be perfectly clear – don't make me repeat everything I say. Take them out and hold them up."

Both women looked at Victor with distaste as they complied. Slowly, and with reluctance that they made no effort to conceal, they drew the plastic organs out of their bodies and held them, glistening with the fluids of their vaginas, up in front of their heaving breasts. Each looked at the other's instrument; both were wet to the point of dripping.

"Okay. Now – I want each of you to sample the other's dildo with your mouth. Suck it a little like you would a prick so you can taste each other's cunt juice. Hell, you've done that before – you ought to enjoy it by now. Well, come on – don't stall every time I tell you to do something. Move!"

Neither woman looked at the man; their eyes were locked on the object in the other's hand. Then Mary reached for the dildo her daughter held. Her arousal was so pronounced that she felt little reluctance to carry out Victor's weird instructions. She took Jessie's dildo and without hesitation brought it up to her face. Mary stared at it for a moment as she studied the wetness of her daughter's vaginal juices at close range, then brought it to her mouth as her tongue slipped out and began to lick the head of the thing that she held in her hand.

"That's it, Mary baby. You like it? You like to suck Jessie's cunt syrup? How does it taste? Taste like her cunt does when you suck it?"

Victor's words only partially registered on Mary's numb brain. But she nodded and widened her pretty eyes as if in surprised pleasure to pacify him as she continued to lick and taste the plastic shaft that had been far up Jessie's vagina… It did have the flavour of her daughter's female essence, and in Mary's present state that made it a highly desirable object.

And Mary's sensual action struck a note in Jessie's lust-fogged mind. She had automatically accepted Mary's dildo when her mother took hers, and Jessie slowly brought it up to her own mouth as she watched Mary savor the object that she now had in her mouth.

But Jessie was never to know the taste of the dildo that Mary had used. As she brought it close to her mouth Victor unexpectedly stopped the perverted tableau.

"Okay, hold it. That's enough of this – I'll pop my rocks if I watch much more of it, and I got a better idea. Gonna let you two finish each other up with your new pricks, and you're gonna do it in a way that'll let ole Victor get his jollies at the same time." He paused and seemed to think as he looked around the room and then back at the two women standing in front of the couch. Both appeared fully dressed; their skirts had fallen back into place as they handled the dildos and only the two pairs of panties on the thick rug suggested that they had partially disrobed.

"Hell, we oughta be in the bedroom, but I don't want to waste the time. We'll do it right here. Right here on the floor. Go on and finish undressing – and don't take all night."

Neither woman had any notion of what he planned next, but neither questioned him. They quickly took off their remaining clothes and then faced him nervously. But both were prepared to carry out his plan, whatever it was, and Mary especially was eager to continue in order to find the relief that she almost desperately needed. Even Jessie's arousal was such that she was willing to continue without protest. She had been initially appalled by the lewd perversion of his schemes, but she was now willing to go ahead with them.

Victor, too, had ripped off the rest of his clothes, and he faced the women of his household with an erection that equalled anything that even the experienced Mary had ever seen.

"Okay, here's what we do. You're gonna fuck each other with the dildo you've got now. I want you on the floor in the sixty-nine position with Mary on top. But don't suck each other – use the dildo. Come on, let's go. You'll be comfortable, Jessie – the carpet's thick and soft."

His remark about the carpet was true, but at this point Jessie would have been unconcerned about bare concrete. Without further urging she sank to the floor in front of the couch and lay down on her back. She looked up at Mary as she brought her knees up and spread them, making her wet vagina visible again to her mother and husband.

"Come on, Mom. I… I'm ready."

And so was Mary. She let her eyes feast briefly on Jessie's exposed crotch, then moved to her and straddled Jessie's chest facing her feet. In another moment she sank to her hands and knees as she brought her shapely bottom over Jessie's upturned face. Both women still held their artificial penis.

"Good. You both look pretty that way. Now take your dildos and work 'em in each other's cunt. We could have used the belt attachments, I guess, but we'll try that later. This time you can just hand fuck each other. Go ahead – get 'em in your pussies."

Both women were willing. They began to work the shafts in between the lips of the other's vagina, and both gave a little soft cry as they simultaneously gave and received pleasure.

"Mom... come a little closer. Can you bend your knees a little and bring your cunt down some more? Yes... oh, that's right. I can get it in easy now. Does that feel nice? OH! Oh gee... Mom, it feels so great when you stick it in my cunt. Go on and shove it in – deep as you can. Oh, damn it feels so perfect. Am I making you feel good?"

Mary mumbled a reply as she worked her dildo into Jessie's young vagina even as the young girl plunged her shaft deep into her mother's body. Each began a series of thrusts, slow at first, into and out of the vagina of the other.

And, unnoticed by the excited females, Victor began to prepare for his own gratification. Holding his penis, he moved around to Jessie's head and sank to his knees just behind Mary's twitching buttocks. His knees were between Mary's spread legs as he leaned over for a close view of his wife's action in her mother's vagina. Jessie became aware of him as her hazy vision finally registered the testicles swinging inches above her forehead.

Victor watched Jessie manipulate the dildo for a moment. It glistened wetly as it was pulled almost out of the grasping lips of Mary's vulva, then pushed back into the eager channel.

"Okay, hold up a minute, Jessie. Keep your prick still in her while I get in her. I'm gonna give her another big bang – while you fuck her cunt with that plastic prick I'm gonna bugger her asshole with a real one. That oughta be a pretty choice double fuck. One of these days you can have it like this too, honey, soon as you loosen up a little… Now hold still while I get my prick in her ass."

Victor paused as he adjusted his position behind Mary's buttocks.

"You got to hold still too, Mary. It's hard enough to hit an asshole without having to worry about a moving target."

Both women were now still as the full implication of Victor's plan hit them. Mary was willing to undergo the double invasion; the perversion involved was, at the moment, insignificant compared to the extra measure of stimulation she would receive.

And Jessie's arousal was such that she looked forward to the act that would take place almost directly in front of her eyes. She would continue to give her mother pleasure in her vagina while she watched her husband's penis derive its own twisted gratification in her rectum.

Jessie's eyes were wide as she watched Victor

bring the tip of his organ to the small brown aperture of Mary's anus. He paused for a moment, then began to push the hard shaft into the crinkled opening. Jessie was fascinated by the lewd sight; she stared as her mother's anal ring involuntarily resisted the unnatural penetration.

"Damn, Mary, don't tense up your asshole like that. You're just making it harder on both of us."

The woman's voice was muffled as she replied without looking back at the man behind her.

"I'm not trying to keep your prick out. I'm relaxing the best I can. You ought to wet your prick with something."

Victor agreed.

"You're right. I should've... say, I'll stick it in your cunt for a minute – no, hell, Jessie's already got her dildo in you."

He rocked back on his knees slightly so that he could look down between Mary's bottom and his flat belly at his wife's flushed face.

"You do it for me, honey. Take it in your mouth – you don't have to suck it, just get it wet so it'll go in your mom's asshole. You won't mind it."

And, strangely, Jessie found that she did not mind. This act, which only a short time ago had so repelled her that it had been largely responsible for their strange arrangement, now seemed natural enough under the circumstances. Jessie's sensual nature had been so developed and

expanded that she now worked the hand that did not hold the dildo up between Mary's buttocks and Victor's thighs to grasp his hard penis. She turned the head down so that it pointed at her face and began to pull gently on it.

"Alright, Victor, I... I'll wet it for you. I don't really mind taking it in my mouth. I'll suck it for a little while if you want me to."

But Jessie's offer was a little late. Her husband's exclamation as his penis throbbed in her hand gave Jessie the first clue.

"Jessie, oh shit – I'm too close – I'm gonna shoot! Take it in your mouth! God – oh God! Squeeze it – pull it! Oh damn, I'm coming... coming... I'm shootin'."

Surprised and unprepared, Jessie nevertheless instinctively pumped on his penis with her little hand as her other hand unconsciously rammed the dildo deeper into her mother's vagina. She stared at the head of Victor's organ with wide eyes, but she did not react fast enough to avoid the first charge of semen as it shot out of his penis and onto her nose and cheek. She let out a little cry as she realized what was happening and turned her pretty face as far to one side as she could. But her position under her mother's spread legs would not allow her to move far enough, and Jessie closed her eyes and whimpered as spurt after spurt of white, glutinous semen shot from her husband's penis to her exposed cheek and ear... and then into her long, raven-black hair.

Chapter 6

Mary was in the best mood she had known for days as she leaned back into the car to pick up the sack of groceries. There was really no reason to be in a cheerful mood; the unwholesome situation in which she and Jessie lived had not changed. But Victor had been out of town on a business trip since the day after the dildo episode, and Jessie was showing signs of seeing the light. The lack of actual participation somehow dulled the edges of her resentment.

And Jessie's expression did nothing to dispel Mary's growing gloom as she entered the apartment.

"Hi, honey. Boy, this sack is heavy. But then it ought to be, I... we've spent a fortune! And all Victor's money, too! Hell, there's gotta be *some* perks to the job," she continued, with a triumphant little smile.

She put the sack on the kitchen cabinet and turned toward Jessie, who sat at the table in the little recessed breakfast nook. Mary was surprised to see three beer cans on the table. "Say, child, that's a lot of beer, for you. Trying to go the alcoholic route?"

Jessie turned grim eyes up to her mother.

"I'd like to. I'd be drinking whisky, except we're out of it. That's something else we have to do – lay in a supply of liquor."

Mary stared at her daughter, well aware now that something was wrong. She stood with one hand still on the sack of groceries.

"Come on now, Jessie, what is it? Something's got you bugged."

Jessie took a sip of beer before she replied, then looked up at the standing woman.

"I'm more than just bugged, Mom. Victor's back; he called from the office. He... Mom, he's got a party on for tonight. Here, with us. What I mean is, we're to entertain the guests he brings home. Men – customers, I guess."

The obviously distressed girl paused.

"Mom... it's to be a fuck party. We'll have to let the men fuck us, just like we were whores hired to take care of his customers for the evening. The bastard – making his family fuck so he can sell some more scribble pads. I hope his damn stationery business goes to hell."

Mary was surprised but not shocked by the news; she had half expected a development of this nature. She abandoned the groceries and slipped into a seat opposite Jessie.

"Baby, are you sure about all this? Did Victor come right out and say."

"That we have to fuck his customers? No, he didn't – I think they were in the office when he called. But there's no mistake. He... he even said to be sure that the dildoes are ready and to hand."

Mary heaved a sigh of quiet resignation.

"Well, I guess that's clear enough. Apparently we're to finally have the pleasure of being fucked by each other – a mother-and-daughter act – with an audience. That sort of depraved circus act ought to sell some office supplies."

She paused, then suddenly feeling bone weary, slowly got to her feet.

"Well, I can see without asking that you're still not ready to get out of all this. If we've got to do it, I'm going to go take a long, hot bath. Maybe I'll fall asleep in the tub and drown No, hell – I'm too mad to go to sleep. Damn!"

Mary turned to leave the kitchen.

"Put the groceries up, Jessie. There's some steak and milk that need to go in the refrigerator."

"Okay, I'll take care of it."

Jessie looked at her mother who, although evidently dispirited, still retained a beauty, grace and elegance that never failed to impress her daughter.

"Mom... mom, you're not mad at me are you? Oh, I know how you must feel – it seems stupid to you for me to stay on with Victor and take all this. I... I have been thinking quite a bit lately about leaving – ever since he made us use the dildos. But somehow I just can't quite do it... yet."

Mary's face softened as she looked at her distressed daughter.

"Okay, honey. You can call the shots; after all it's your marriage. But I think it's a losing battle. Well, I'm for the tub and a long soak. Maybe you ought to order the liquor while we're thinking about it."

* * *

The atmosphere was more than just a little strained; Jessie knew as she looked at the girls that they had had sex with her husband. Well, by his standards, perhaps that was only a small thing.

"I... I'm sorry. Didn't mean to just leave you standing there. Come on in. Victor's not with you?"

The lush brunette smiled.

"He's out picking up the men. Seems they're staying at three different motels, for some reason. I'm Betty Anderson, your husband's secretary, and this is Jill Feinberg. She's been with the company about a month. Another girl will be arriving soon – she doesn't work at Jordan's Stationery, but she's going to freelance for us tonight."

The pretty young girl smiled.

"I'm so glad to know you, Mrs. Jordan. I wasn't really sure that we'd ever meet."

Jessie studied the young redhead. She was sure that this was the girl Victor had mentioned hiring for public relations' purposes. Well, hell – he had apparently married largely for the same purpose.

Jessie waved a hand toward the empty living room.

"Sit down. My mother will be in in a minute. I... she'll be in on the party with us, as I suppose you know. Want something to drink?"

Betty shook her head.

"Not yet. I imagine there will be all the liquor we can handle a little later."

Jill Feinberg giggled.

"Nothing for me, thanks. My mother says I'm too young to drink, and I think she's right. But she hasn't said anything about fucking and smoking pot so I guess that's all right."

Jessie looked sharply at the girl with a sense of mild irritation. Her lewd language made it clear that she was well aware of the evening's basic purpose. Suddenly the young wife felt a desire for as much information as she could get. Victor's secretary had known him a lot longer than she had, and probably even more intimately.

She sat down on the couch by the pretty brunette. Her eyes went briefly over the girl's full figure; it was the voluptuous type that Victor liked. Then she looked up into the girl's cool eyes.

"Betty... I wonder... well, I wonder if you could tell me a little about this part of Victor's business. This is all new to me. These parties for his customers, I mean. Have you... well, have you been in on them before?"

The girl's smile was thin, but her tone seemed friendly. "Oh yes, a good many times. Too many for my liking, actually. And Jill has entertained several times; in fact this is her principal duty."

Jessie felt foolish as she flushed slightly.

"Well, what I'm really getting at, I guess, is what these affairs are really like. I mean, what goes on exactly?"

Betty looked steadily at the young wife as she felt a curious mixture of sympathy and contempt. She knew that Jessie really knew the score; that she was merely grasping at straws to find some kind of reassurance that the evening wouldn't turn out to be as hellish as she imagined. But Betty also knew that Jessie had not understood the situation when she married Victor, and it was a pretty rough thing for a young bride to be subjected to...

"Mrs. Jordan – Jessie – I think you really know. We are here in the capacity of 'company hostesses', in other words, strictly for the pleasure of the men. To put it bluntly, so that they can fuck us. Or whatever they want to do; I'm afraid that usually fucking is a fairly small part of it. For instance Victor tells me that he tried to get a specially trained for tonight – but thank god, he failed. I've never been quite sure why, but men seem to get a big bang out of seeing a girl fucked by a dog. Personally speaking, I don't much care for it – I'm always afraid the dog will get hung up in my cunt like they do sometimes when they screw a bitch. Dog type bitch, that is.

But so far it hasn't happened to me. Of course I have only taken on a dog just a few times. And I have to admit that they usually give me a good come."

Jessie, wide-eyed with apprehension, now felt a little sick; her desire for information had evaporated.

"I... I see. Well, if you two won't have anything I think I'll have quick one. I feel like I'm going to need it."

The bell chimed once more. This time, Jessie's mother answered the door to an attractive, smartly-dressed woman in her late twenties. Mary could not help but be impressed by her confident manner and sophisticated appearance. She felt an unexpected empathy for the woman.

"Hello, my name is Bridget. Bridget O'Connor. I've come to help with the party that Victor Jordan is throwing here tonight."

"Please, come in... we're trying to get things ready."

* * *

"Hey – that stuff ready?

The voice in the kitchen door made Mary look up as she put the finishing touches on a tray of sandwiches.

"It's ready, Victor. Victor... come in a minute and close the door. Please."

Her son-in-law frowned slightly but did as she asked.

"What is it, Mary? I need to get back out there – you do too. It's been a little slow so far. We got to get a little life in this thing."

Mary faced the man she had come to despise.

"Victor – what exactly do you want us to do? Jessie, I mean. Can't you go easy on her? After all, she is your wife. And you've got three other women."

The man shook his head impatiently.

"Oh hell, Mary, don't start this crap. The fact that Jessie's my wife adds a lot of spice for a couple of those bastards out there. They've always wanted to try wife swapping and have never had the nerve, and they're thinking that at least they're gonna get to fuck somebody's wife. Hell, Jessie'll be okay. Don't worry about it. Come on – let's get those sandwiches out there. Two or three of them didn't have any dinner, and it's always such hell to fuck on an empty stomach..."

* * *

Jessie's walk was a little unsteady as she carried the two martini glasses. She had already had more to drink than she usually allowed herself in an entire evening. She just felt that she was going to need it although, so far, the party had been surprisingly mild.

"Here, Jessie. You're about to pass me up. Don't do that."

The young wife turned and stared at the balding, paunchy man on the couch. He was right – he was the one she had volunteered to get a drink for.

"Oh, sorry, Mr.... Mr...?"

"Eddie, honey, call me Eddie. I know your mom. Pretty well, as it happens. Here, sit down by me. You look a little wobbly."

Jessie sided in relief as she slumped down beside the smiling man. She saw his eyes go to her legs as the short skirt went high on her lush thighs... probably over the tops of her stockings, but she was too woozy to care. She quivered slightly as she felt one of his hands on her leg.

"Jessie, honey – you're the sexiest little thing I've seen in a long time. When the fucking starts I want your cunt first – okay?"

The bluntness of his proposal sobered the pretty young Amerasian slightly, but only for a moment. She smiled at him. He was a nice man – why shouldn't he fuck her first?

"Okay, Mr. – I mean, Eddie, if you want to. I guess it's all right for you fuck me first. Say, maybe you shouldn't fuck me at all. Don't you have a wife?"

The man chuckled.

"Sure do, honey, but that don't make no difference. You got a husband, too, don't you? He's the one told me how nice and tight your cunt is. You know, maybe I ought to check it out a little."

Before the befuddled girl recognized the

man's intention he leaned toward her and ran a sweaty hand in between her soft thighs. The fingers travelled without difficulty up to the band of her panties as Jessie spread her legs slightly in an automatic reflex to his touch. Then she reacted and clamped her thighs against his inquiring hand.

"Oh... no, you shouldn't!" she said, illogically. "That's not nice... I mean... my husband is here – he'll see you. Please – take your hand away. You shouldn't touch me like that."

The man looked up at her impatiently. He was willing to put up with a minimum amount of apparent reluctance, but any real objection from one of the girls would be intolerable. He went along with her for the moment.

"Hell, Jessie, you don't mind my hand. Let me finger fuck you a little – make you feel good. I know a finger ain't like a prick up your cunt, but..."

Jessie's alcohol befuddled mind rebelled. Her reaction to the drinks she had consumed was opposite to the usual one; instead of loosening her morals it tended to destroy the careful rationalizations with which she meant to justify her part in the evening's lewd activities.

"No – no, you shouldn't try to play with me like that. It's not right. My... my husband is right over there."

The paunchy man's limited tolerance vanished.

"You damn right he's there. He's the one

bragged about what good pussy you are."

He turned toward Victor, who stood with Betty in a small group at the bar.

"Hey, Victor – comm'ere. Thought your wife was good cunt, just like her mom was at the motel that night. Hell, she don't even wanna finger fuck. What the hell?"

The man's loud complaint brought Jessie to her senses. She realized that she had been uncooperative, despite her earlier decision to comply with Victor's wishes. It dawned on her for the first time that she was actually a little afraid of her husband.

"What's the problem, Eddie? Jessie not treating you right? She will, I'll guarantee it. Maybe she's had a little more to drink than she should."

Victor turned to Jessie. His smile was not pleasant.

"Now honey, you're gonna be nice to Eddie, aren't you baby? Yes?" As she nodded meekly, his voice dropped an octave to a threatening snarl. "You're damn right you are. You read me, Jessie?"

Face down, looking at the floor, Jessie nodded once more. She understood him clearly enough, and she recognized the implied threat in his tone. Damn, if she was going to cooperate it was stupid to cause trouble before she did it. She composed her features and looked up again with a sweet smile.

"Victor... yes, darling, I read you. I... Eddie

misunderstood me, I think. I'll do whatever he wants me to. I... I want to do it. Please, honey – I'll cooperate."

Victor looked at his young wife closely.

"I know you will, Jessie."

He paused and then smiled at the man seated by his lovely wife.

"She'll be okay, Eddie. Drinks may have got to her for a minute; she's not used to so much alcohol. Tell you what – we'll have her prove it to you. What would like to have her do? Anything you like."

The man seemed to be appeased. The thought of having this lush young girl at his disposal quickly erased his displeasure. He stared down at her lithe, yet curvaceous body and grinned.

"Well now, Victor, I don't exactly know. Lots of things she could do, I guess. Hey – does she like to double fuck?"

Victor grinned.

"At the moment she likes to do anything. What kind of a double fuck you have in mind?"

The man seemed eager now.

"Well, maybe just a quick, stand-up deal here where everybody can see. Sandwich style – her in the middle between you and me. One of us in her cunt and the other in her asshole. How's that sound?"

Victor was not wildly enthusiastic about the proposal; it was not the way he had planned to start the activity. But, hell – it was as good a way as any. He could save the movies until later when everybody was trying to catch a second wind. Besides, there was no real alternative without risking the man's displeasure. And it happened that he was the most important customer in the group.

"Sure, Eddie, why not? Sounds good to me. And I bet it does to Jessie, too. right, darling?"

The look in Victor's eyes as he turned to his wife made her range of choice clear.

"I… yes, Victor. Anything you say. I'll be glad to… accommodate Eddie."

The man's good humour returned. He exploded with laughter at Jessie's reply.

"Hey, honey, you sure talk sweet. But I don't wanna 'accommodate', I wanna fuck. That mean the same thing, baby? Tell me if it does – tell me you want me to fuck you. Go on, baby – I wanna hear you say it."

Victor grinned down at his young wife as she sat before him on the couch. He welcomed her discomfort; it served her right for incurring the man's displeasure. And now that he thought of it, the man's proposal seemed more and more attractive.

"Well, go on, Jessie – tell the gentlemen that you want him to fuck you. Tell him how you'd like for him to do it."

Jessie felt herself flush bright red as the whole room now seemed to be focussed on her and what she would say in return. She turned to the man at her side and forced herself to speak, but her voice was barely audible.

"I… I do want you to fuck me. However you want to. If you want to double fuck me with my husband, I'll be glad."

Victor cut her off.

"Speak up, Jessie, nobody can hear you."

He paused as an idea struck him, then turned to the scattered group of people.

"Hey, everybody – give me your attention. Everybody – please."

He waited for a minute until the buzz of conversation died and the group turned to look at the trio at the couch. Victor was grinning as he held up a hand.

"Come on over here, if you will. My wife has something to say that I think you'll find interesting. That's it – come in a little closer. I had planned some movies to start the ball rolling, but I think my sweet little slut of a wife wants to do it instead."

Victor looked down at the increasingly nervous young girl he had married.

"Alright, darling – tell them about it. About what Eddie proposed, and what you're going to do. Speak up so everybody can hear you. I know they'll be interested. Go ahead."

Jessie felt numb, but she knew that Victor would not tolerate less than full cooperation. But, God – how could he expect her to talk of such things before all these people? Then she moaned inwardly as it struck her that he wanted her not only to talk but also to perform in front of them. He wanted not only for her to serve as a whore, but to do it without the privacy in which a respectable whore plied her profession. But, as usual since this whole unholy mess began, she had no choice.

Jessie drew a deep breath and faced the group, most of whom were now close to the couch and obviously eager for the act which would kick off the evening's fun. She made herself smile, and somehow she found it easier to talk than she had anticipated.

"Well, I... I want Eddie and Victor to – well, to double fuck me – one in my cunt and the other in my asshole. I've never done it, but it ought to be wonderful for the girl. I think we're to do it standing up – me between them. I don't know who will take my cunt and who will fuck me in my asshole, but it doesn't really matter."

Jessie paused and looked up at her husband.

"Is that alright, honey? Is that the way you want to do it?"

The man at her side answered before Victor could speak.

"That's just right, baby. In fact it's more than just right! And I'm ready to fuck – right now. See what you done?"

He took Jessie's hand and pressed it in the crotch of his trousers, then humped his hips slightly under her hand in a lewd gesture that expressed his intentions graphically. And, to her surprise, Jessie felt a certain warmth in her loins as her fingers tested the almost hard penis through the man's clothes. He seemed adequately equipped for the job he intended to do… damn, his penis was as big as Victor's. Jessie's mind churned as it occurred to her that it would be better to have a smaller organ in her rectum.

But she had little time for such thoughts. Both men were now eager to begin, and the rest of the crowd was impatient for the start of the promised action. And, by no means least, Jessie was herself ready, at least in the physical sense.

Victor seemed to take charge. He held out a hand to his pretty wife.

"Stand up, honey, and get your clothes off. Time to fuck. Eddie, let's you and me strip, too. You as ready as I am?"

The man beside Jessie chuckled as he picked up his drink and finished it, then got to his feet.

"More ready, I bet, Victor. You've had a lot of Jessie's pussy before, but it's new stuff to me. Which side you want me to take?"

Victor laughed.

"You're the guest here, Eddie. Take your choice. You're welcome to my wife's cunt or her asshole, whichever you want. In fact you can have 'em both over the course of the evening."

Both men were quickly undressing as they talked, but the eyes of the spectators saw only

Jessie's disrobing operation. The chore was a brief one; she wore no underclothes except her already moist bikini panties. That wispy material soon joined her skirt on one end of the couch, and she felt a stab of sensual excitement as she turned, nude except for garter belt and hose, to face the two naked men and the crowd behind them.

The crowd was impressed; they all seemed enthralled by Jessie's tall, lithe young body; they ogled her superbly full, pointed breasts, her flat tummy and the tantalising 'vee' of her thick, luxuriant bush that nestled at the apex of her long, shapely legs. At the edge of the group, Mary was surprised by the obvious power of her daughter's femininity over this fairly jaded bunch.

"Fuck me slowly, look at them tits."

"Tits, hell. Look at that cunt. Boy I bet that little thing's tight and juicy."

"Turn round sweetheart, let's see your ass..."

Victor seemed proud of the impact his wife had on the assembly. He put his hands on her shoulders and turned her gently so that she faced the people squarely, then shook her shoulders just enough to make the lush globes of her tip-tilted breasts quiver. He moved his hands down to the soft flesh and tweaked the already hard nipples.

"Victor... hey, ole buddy, I can't wait."

The sudden hoarseness of Eddie's voice

reflected his anxiety.

"These other jokers can get their rocks off in Jessie later, if they want. Right now I got to fuck her. Victor, if it's okay with you I'll take her cunt and you can have her asshole. Think we're near enough the right height?"

The man's words focused Victor's attention on the act immediately at hand, and he found himself almost as aroused as the man who was about to sample Jessie for the first time. The act they proposed was perverted enough to arouse Victor fully. He had become aware, in recent months, that his response to routine sex had tapered off noticeably, and that increasingly offbeat situations were necessary to arouse him fully. The development had been of some concern to him, but he had managed to keep sexually occupied in a variety of ways that partially masked the problem.

"Suits me, Eddie. Okay Jessie, right here. Face Eddie – that's it. Now, let's see."

Victor backed off slightly to appraise the geometrical problem involved. The trouble with a lot of these three and four way deals was that they didn't work out in practice like they sounded in conversation, usually because the people involved just didn't fit properly. But in this case...

"Eddie, we can make this work. You and me are about the same height and that's the important thing. Jessie is too short for us, but we can fix that."

He turned to the ring of spectators.

"One of you jokers get me three or four thick books off the shelves over there. I knew having a library would be useful sooner or later."

One of the men secured the necessary volumes and brought them to Victor.

"Ought to do it. Thanks. Jessie... stand on these and let's see what we got."

The young wife dutifully stepped up on the mound of books and again faced her anxious client. Her eyes automatically dropped to his loins to check the condition of his penis, and she was gratified to see that the brief delay had had no adverse effects.

"Okay, looks good. For me, anyway – how bout you, Eddie? Is Jessie's cunt about the right height for you to fuck?"

The man stared at the barely visible lips of Jessie's vagina as they nestled beneath the protection of her black pubic curls.

"I think so. But I'll damn sure find out... you ready, Victor?"

Victor nodded as he reached out and fondled his young wife's lush buttocks.

"All set back here. Tell you what, Eddie – I think I better get in her ass first. She's not used to it, and it's gonna hurt a little. She'll have to bend over while I put it in, then she can straighten up to take your prick."

Eddie nodded.

"Okay, what ever you say. I'll check her tits out while she's bent over."

Victor chuckled.

"Good deal."

He patted Jessie's soft buttocks again as she stood before him on the books.

"Okay, honey, time to bugger. You'll like this after you get used to it. Bend over and reach back and spread your ass for me."

He paused and looked around as Jessie bent before him.

"Mary."

Mary had anticipated him. She appeared at Victor's side holding a jar of petroleum jelly.

"Here, Victor. Use a lot of this; Jessie'll need it."

Victor grinned as he reached for the jar, then he seemed to change his mind.

"You do it, Mary. Put the stuff on my prick and up Jessie's asshole." Then, turning to the little group that crowded around them with an easy laugh, "It's what mom's are for, isn't it?"

The pretty woman did not bother to comment. She took a generous amount of the greasy substance on her fingers and brought them to his waving penis. She felt it throb in anticipation as she rubbed the lubricant on the hard shaft.

"Okay, honey – don't jack it off. I want to blow my first load up Jessie's bottom. Put some in her ass if you're going to."

Mary again hooked a finger into the jar and brought a glob of the substance out. She looked down at Jessie, who was still bent forward with her hands pulling open her luscious buttocks.

"Honey, I'm going to put some of this in you. It'll help a lot."

She brought her finger to the crease between her daughter's spread buttocks and to the grey-pink puckered opening of her anus. After a moment she felt Jessie shudder as her finger invaded the tight little opening… She rubbed the lubricant into the clenched, quivering channel with the thought that the entry of Victor's big penis would be difficult and probably very painful the first time.

But the situation took an unexpected turn. Eddie looked over her shoulder at Victor.

"Say, Victor… I think I'll take a rain check on this. I guess it seems funny, but instead of startin' like this I think I'd like to see the mother fuck your wife. I mean, I still want to fuck her, but I'm not really too hot on this standin' up bit. Okay with you if we have the mother-daughter act first, then I do it?"

Victor looked at the man in surprise. Such a change was the very last thing that he wanted. At this point Victor wanted only to get his penis safely into Jessie's enticing little anus, but Eddie was the customer, and his wishes would have to prevail. Damn it, customer or not the bastard shouldn't have started this episode unless he intended to finish it.

But Victor made his smile and voice mask his real feelings.

"Sure, Eddie – anything you say. Want me to put the mother on now or wait till later?"

The man grinned sheepishly – in a way that gave Victor an insight into the real problem.

"Well, why don't we wait a little? Maybe it's a little early yet for the main act."

"Sure, Eddie. That's a good idea. Anytime you're ready to see Jessie's mom fuck her, you just holler."

Victor forced himself not to look at the other man's crotch; but he already knew that the real problem was that Eddie had, for some reason, lost his erection. Damn, Victor thought, that poor bastard's in bad shape when he goes soft right before he fucks Jessie.

* * *

My god, thought Mary, as she felt the man's cock slide up her cum-slick ass in one smooth motion, here we go again. She had been so busy sucking the rigid cock that she now caressed with her saliva-slick fingers that she hadn't even suspected that her out-thrust buttocks would have presented such an irresistibly tempting target to a roving male. And at first, she didn't know who it was. Now, looking over her shoulder she saw Eddie, the older man who had tried to fuck Jessie in her ass and had fucked her in the motel with Bill, his partner in crime. Oh well, where he failed with the daughter, he's now succeeding with the mother. Eddie was rough. He lacked finesse he'd shown the first time she had met him.

"Hey… go easy, lover. That's my asshole you're fucking. And your cock isn't small." With a secret smile, Mary was tempted to add 'any more' but thought better of it.

Eddie just laughed and fucked her harder.

Mary's whole body bucked with Eddie's violent thrusts. She felt the hard, plundering pole of flesh deep inside her rectal cavity, causing her unknown sensations as it burrowed ever deeper into her bowels. In an utterly masochistic way she began to enjoy being the fuck-toy of strange men, of being used so savagely like some cheap prostitute… it was strangely liberating. It wasn't like the time with him and Bill in the motel. Back then there had been some sort of weird rapport between the three of them. But this… this was different. Anonymous. Impersonal. She was now officially an orgiast. A fuck-slave, to be used and abused at will. She felt hand of Bill, whose cock she was fellating, come down on the back of her head in a silent command for her to resume sucking him. Mary obliged without protest.

Eddie laughed when he saw this and said, "Yeah, the little Chinese lady likes that, doesn't she… likes sucking cock and taking it up the ass at the same time. Just like we did before."

His partner in the act only groaned in blissful acknowledgment as Mary ran her tongue around his bell-shaped glans and let it flutter briefly over its string-like frenulum.

The elegant 38-year-old glanced sideways

across the room and took in the scene in a few brief moments. The first person she saw, just inches away from her, was Jill, the little redhead whore who was doing just what Mary was doing, almost a mirror image. Not a bad technique, either. I could learn a few tricks from that little cock-sucking strumpet, she thought. The object of Jill's attentions was also being teasingly kissed by the lovely Bridget O'Connor in all her naked glory. Oh Lord, for some reason that woman turns me on, mused Mary.

Beyond this little group her daughter and Betty were avidly mouthing a kneeling male's stiff erection. She watched in wonder as Victor's voluptuous secretary 'stole' the prize from her daughter and then reluctantly let her have it again. But Jessie couldn't be feeling too deprived, her mother reasoned. She too was being fucked energetically from behind. Victor lay back on the sofa and watched the debauch of his pretty young wife with a decadent, scowling expression that marred his good looks. All this and he doesn't look happy. Just a little drunk. Mary almost felt sorry for him.

Eddie was close now. He redoubled his efforts and Mary had to be careful not to bite the cock she was sucking. She, too, felt a climax approaching, felt her cunt tingle with pre-orgasmic shudders. She knew that she had reached the last plateau before the peak. It was only a matter of time.

Above her Bill grunted and the beautiful

Chinese woman's mouth was flooded by jets of thick semen. Behind her Eddie gasped as he, too, unloaded his cum in convulsive spurts deep inside her rectum. Jessie's lovely mother reared up and climaxed with explosive little staccato gasps, her eyes closed in ecstasy and her mouth half-open in a silent scream. Long, sticky white strands connected her lips to the swollen cockhead she held in her hand.

Mary felt a hand caress her cheek. She felt soft lips on her own and a warm, wet tongue enter her mouth. She opened her eyes in surprise to find Bridget O'Connor was kissing her with a tenderness and passion she had never experienced before.

Jill Feinberg was not happy. In the absence of a real dog, they had decided to cast the perky young redhead in that role. Entirely naked but for a studded collar and a lead, she was told to crawl on all fours. To complete her humiliation, she was forced to wear a strap-on dildo and Victor had thrust a strange device in her ass, shaped like a plug so that it wouldn't easily fall out, with a brush-like tail attached.

"Easy girl... easy. There. How you like that pussy? I bet that's the prettiest you've ever had. You're a lucky dog, you know that?"

To the uproarious welcome of the male visitors, Victor led his 'dog' by it's lead.

From her kneeling position, Jessie looked over her shoulder back towards the 'dog' at her heels. On the thick-piled carpet of the living room floor with the entire group crowded around, she was reluctantly preparing herself to provide the feature attraction of what had been a long evening. She had lost track of the men who had taken her, and of the various ways that they had done it. Only the numbing and welcome effects of alcohol had enabled her to endure the ordeal psychologically. Physically she had responded well enough. Too well, in fact – her uninhibited response was a source of increasing concern as her liquor clouded mind began to clear. And now this – the ultimate degradation.

Victor grinned down at his prone wife.

"You're lucky, honey, this pooch is as hot as hell. He hasn't had a piece of ass for as long as anyone can remember. You're gonna get quite a fucking."

He turned to the people crowded around both sides of the prostrated woman. They were all nude, and most of them had already engaged in multiple acts of sex. All but two of the men had taken Jessie in one way or another in the past three hours, and the group as a whole had been about satiated. But the perverted nature of the act about to take place between a young girl and a make-believe dog had reawakened their interest.

"Want him to lick your cunt first, Jess? It ought to be so full of come that he'll have to get some of it out to have room to get his prick in. How about it – want the doggie to lick your cunt?"

Jessie briefly closed her eyes in a symbolic attempt to blot out the scene. To her dismay, her mind was clearing, and as the alcohol induced haze dissolved the full dimensions of her perversion and degradation began to become apparent. And yet she had no choice – no way to avoid the monstrous act that her husband was forcing on her.

"I... I don't care. I guess he can if he wants to. Whatever you say..."

The spectators had more positive opinions.

"Yeah, Victor, let 'the dog' lick her first. I think I fucked Jessie last; we'll see how he likes my come."

"Hell, Larry, you're crazy – you fucked Jessie in her asshole. I was the last one to blow my load in her cunt."

Jessie tried to shut out the vulgar comments as she waited for her redheaded lover. Damn, if only the alcohol effects hadn't worn off just when she needed them the most.

She forced herself to open her eyes and look at the girl between her legs. Part of her rejoiced in this pushy little slut's humiliation. But the idea of any woman other than her mother as a female sex partner... was disturbing.

And there was no longer much doubt about it. Jessie stiffened as she felt Jill's lively little tongue make contact with the lips of her vagina. Instinctively she arched her back and thrust her bottom higher into the air to give her better access. But the girl did not concentrate immediately on the center of her sex; instead she transferred his attentions temporarily to the soft and sensitive flesh of her inner thighs. Jill the dog licked the white skin thoroughly as Jessie involuntarily raised her bottom even higher and even reached back to spread her ass cheeks wider so as to give her easier access to her ultimate goal.

She did not tarry long on the secondary areas; after he had both inner thighs glistening with the wetness of her tongue the teenager again went to her sensitive labia and her swollen, reddened asshole. She licked vertically up the half-closed, seeping lips, then, with an adroitness that could only have come from experience, penetrated and separated the soft, fleshy flaps with a knowing tongue.

In spite of herself Jessie could not but react to the perverted stimulation. She tried to muffle her little moans as she buried her head in her folded arms and closed her eyes. Her buttocks started to flex and quiver as she began to enjoy the younger girl's attention. Damn, dog or no dog, that little slut really did know how to lick, how to use that long, soft tongue just like a dog would.

"Look at her lick. Boy, she won't even want a man to eat her pussy after she gets through."

"Hey, Betty – you gettin' hot for some 'dog' fucking? He'll probably have plenty left for the rest of you girls. Damn, look at that big prick. Biggest pooch prick I *ever* saw!"

The ribald comments of the spectators reflected the reawakening of their desires as they watched the pretty young wife submit to the make-believe animal. And the women were affected as much as the men; even Mary, standing unobtrusively at the back of the group found herself unwillingly stimulated as she watched a human 'dog' make love to her daughter. The last remark made her attention focus on the artificial penis, suitably made of red rubber, as it dangled between the redhead's thighs. It was huge - at least ten inches long. Mary's pulse raced as she looked at the shaft – how would a thing like that feel in a woman's vagina? For an instant she almost envied Jessie.

This emotion was considerably heightened when the man standing next to her casually reached behind her and slipped a finger into her own sperm-dripping pussy.

And then Mary's participation in the act increased from the level of spectator to that of participant. She had not noticed that Victor had turned and was searching the group of a dozen or so partygoers.

"Mary – there you are. Come on up here, dear mother-in-law, and help your daughter get fucked. Come on up."

Mary found herself moving toward the little group. She was nude, as was everyone, but she was so preoccupied that she was not conscious of the sensual bounce of her heavy breasts as she went over to the smaller group.

But at least one of the spectators noticed.

"Hot damn – look at them boobs shake. Easy to see where Jessie got her tits from. Hey, Victor – is Mary's cunt as good as Jessie's?"

Victor grinned at the questioner.

"Nelson, ole buddy, I'm not gonna answer that. Why you think I got both of 'em here tonight? You probably already fucked Jessie – fuck Mary and see for yourself. Or are you through for the night?"

The crowd laughed as Victor turned to his mother-in-law, who had been unable to stop herself from blushing at the shameful, yet nonetheless deeply erotic, way that she was being offered around like the way you offer candy to visiting kids.

"Mary, honey, want you to help a little. You take young Jill... I mean Fido's... prick and play with it a little to be sure it's in the best possible condition for your daughter. Then I'm gonna let you help our pooch get it in Jessie's cunt."

Mary made no reply as she stared at the long organ. She was now so aroused that her new role was not unwelcome. She sank to her knees beside Jill and put a hand on her back as she watched the teenager work on Jessie's dripping vagina, her little pink tongue now flicking in and out of the puffed lips and even fluttering over the distended anal sphincter. The thought occurred to Mary that, unlike a real dog, this one was apparently quite aware of a girl's clitoris and other erogenous zones, judging by the way her daughter was twisting and writhing so dramatically, yet never moving out of range of her persecutor's mouth.

"Okay, Mary – quit daydreaming and take that prick. Remember, you're doing it for Jessie as well as the dog."

Victor's words snapped the Chinese beauty's attention back to her job and she bent slightly to look again at the swaying organ beneath the girl's rounded little belly.

Mary moved one hand slowly toward the strange penis. Then she grasped it almost eagerly; the erotic nature of the situation had her own loins once more juicy and aroused, and her touch on the girl's dildo provoked a seemingly mutual reaction.

For the Jill did react; Mary's fingers made her abandon for a moment the succulent, sperm-sodden vagina in front of her and turn her drink- and drug-glazed eyes to look at the pretty Oriental who seemed so interested in her artificial penis. This interest was not a new one for Jill; despite her tender age, she was no stranger to being touched by one of her own sex.

"Okay, Mary – doggie's prick feel like it's ready?"

Mary did not look up at Victor, but she entered into the spirit of this gross charade.

"This dog's ready. I think he can fuck Jessie now."

"Good. Mary, I'm gonna let you help him

get it in. You'll have to move him up and get his paws round Jessie's waist. He'll know what to do – he's done it before."

At this there was a great deal of ribald laughter from the men, who were at last entering into the spirit of the bizarre piece of theatre that was being played out before them.

For the first time Mary looked up at her daughter's face. Although – or perhaps because – her eyes were screwed shut, she saw there an expression that reflected a lust that seemed to equal her own. Mary had a fleeting rational thought – at least Jessie seemed to be aroused and ready in a purely sexual sense for the ordeal. But her reaction later might be something else again.

Her mind snapped back to the details of the coming union as Jill Feinberg began to move up on Jessie's kneeling body. She sprung up on her back with a little bound, looking more like some demented female chimpanzee rather than any sort of dog, her arms almost meeting as they gripped under her belly, and somehow Mary's hand stayed on the dildo as she encouraged the move. The organ felt strange in her fingers, and gave the impression of being at the same time both harder and softer than a flesh and blood penis. But it seemed to jerk authentically enough in her grasp, and Mary had no doubt that it would provide exquisite pleasure to Jessie. For a moment she envied her excited daughter.

Victor looked down at his wife.

"You ready, Jessie? You want the doggie's prick up your cunt? Tell me if you want him to fuck you."

Jessie's eyes were closed but her answer was not hesitant.

"Oh, yes… yes. Let the dog fuck me, if that's what you want."

Her husband shook his head.

"I didn't ask you what *I* want. I want to know if you want the dog to fuck you. Tell me exactly what you want."

Again Jessie's answer tumbled out without hesitation.

"Yes – damn it, I want him. Let him fuck me – I want his big doggie prick up my cunt. Oh, hell – Mom, put it in for me. Hurry – I want Jill… I mean… the dog… to fuck me."

Jessie's words made Mary act. The 'dog' was now in position, and she once more grasped the long rubber penis as she sought to line it up with the top of Jessie's waiting labial split, just below her anal star. The girl's earlier attentions had left her daughter's pretty flushed lips separated and ready.

As Mary slid the head of the rubber phallus into her daughter's upturned cuntal groove with one hand, with her other she gave a little slap to Jill's pert bottom and the young girl immediately pushed the big red organ into Jessie's channel. Mary was surprised at the speed of the initial thrust as she felt the shaft slide in her hand and enter her daughter's willing vagina with

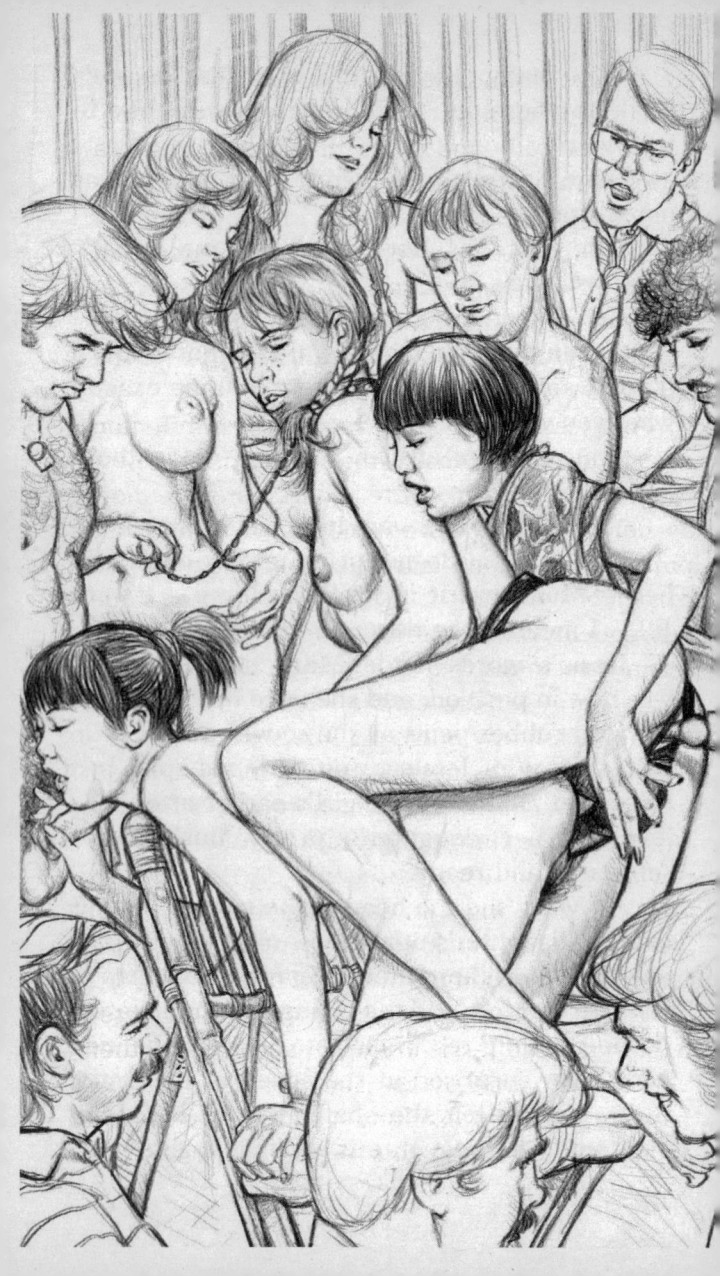

an almost inaudible 'schlooop'. She barely had time to remove her hand before the 'dog' penetrated fully and then immediately began a series of rapid strokes.

Mary rocked back on her knees as the girl began to fuck Jessie. Her tempo was faster than that of the normal human act and she could see Jessie tremble and quiver under the strange impetus. But she could also tell that the young wife was experiencing pleasure.

And Jessie was being gripped by a stimulation of a kind and intensity that was entirely new to her. Her moans were clearly audible now as her head rolled from side to side and her pink tongue wiped a trickle of saliva from the corner of her mouth. As if in the grip of some weird delusion, or perhaps because she really *wanted* to think that she was on the receiving end of some violent canine rutting, she started to babble a litany of crazed lust.

"Oh, God… I never – fuck me, fuck me. I never knew. Mom, are you there? He's fucking my cunt. The damn dog's fucking me. God, he fucks fast – and it's so fucking *big*! I'm gonna come! I'm coming! Oh, damn – damn! Fuck me. You damn dog, fuck me! Pump that big cock inside me! I'm coming… oh, oh *ohhhhh*…!"

Mary was still on her knees by her daughter as she watched Jessie's climax. The girl's mother was almost awed by the speed and severity of her daughter's orgasm and it suddenly occurred to her that a real dog, too, might have something very special for Jessie.

And then it seemed that she might have the opportunity to find out for herself. Jill pulled her organ out of Jessie's battered but fulfilled vagina just as Victor, who had been taken by surprise by the brevity of the intercourse, recovered his wits. He looked at the crowd.

"Hey, that was pretty quick, wasn't it? Well, I guess it figures – it's hard to get a good class of dog these days. Tell you what – if you'd like to see Fido in action a little more we could have 'him' fuck Jessie's mother. Mary's right here and handy, and I bet she'd like a little pooch prick up her cunt. How about it – anybody like to see that?"

There was a general murmur of approval from the group, and Victor could see that their interest in this particular area of sex was far from satisfied. In short, they wanted to see this elegant Chinese lady 'dog'-fucked.

He turned to the lovely nude woman on her knees by his wife. "What do you say, Mary? Like to take Fido on?"

Mary was somewhat dazed by the combination of alcohol and perverted sex as she turned to the grinning man. Once again she had little choice, but in addition her aroused body called out for relief. Watching Jessie's experience had given her a desire she had never known before...

"Okay, Victor... if I must."

Victor laughed nastily.

"Hear that? I figured my sweet, sexy mother-in-law would want a little dog prick after she saw what it did to Jessie. Okay, Mary – the pooch is all yours."

But Eddie wasn't to be so easily cheated out of his preferred fantasy.

"Say, you haven't forgotten what you promised earlier?"

He paused again and then grinned.

"Let's see… why don't we have Jessie fuck her mom in the ass while she takes the pooch's prick up her cunt?"

There was a murmur of approval from the crowd. But Mary was thunderstruck by Eddie's proposal. There was a limit to what she would or would not do in front of a bunch of perverted stationery buyers – and for heaven's sake, this was just going too far.

"No! God damn it – no. I won't do it – no more of this perverted crap."

Her eyes were blazing as she looked directly at her son-in-law.

"Victor, you bastard – you can go to hell and take all your damn customers with you. I'm not your whore – find somebody else for them to fuck if that's what you want. You hear me? Go to hell, you slimy bastard."

Tears streamed from her eyes as Mary got to her feet. She looked down at her shocked daughter, who now lay on her belly, her lovely long raven hair fanned out around her head.

"Jessie, baby – I've had it. No more of

this for me, I'm leaving this zoo. Do you want to come with me, or stay here and let these bastards fuck you some more so that your depraved husband can sell a few more reams of typing paper? Victor'll probably let you suck his prick, since I won't do it. Jessie – *are you coming with me?*"

But the young girl seemed paralyzed. Her mouth was open but she said nothing as she looked at her mother through wild, appalled eyes. And Mary read the answer to her questions in those eyes; suddenly she knew from her daughter's expression the terrible realisation had dawned upon Jessie that she had finally joined the enemy: she had converted to Victor's perverted way of life.

Mary started to talk to Jessie, to plead with her. But a flash of insight told her that the effort would be futile. Instead she turned to Victor, who was, for once, also speechless in surprise, and spat on him. The act was an affirmation of her contempt for the man, a tiny gesture of humiliation in front of his cronies and clients and a symbolic cleansing of her mouth that had been the receptacle for so much male sperm over the last few weeks.

But her son in law was not going to let her rain on his parade: even as she ran sobbing from the room, Mary heard Victor's laugh boom out.

"Well, how about that? Isn't that just like a nagging mother-in-law? Still, hate to lose Mary – she really was a great fuck. Guess you'll just have to fuck twice as hard now, Jessie baby."

Only one person seemed to react to Mary's tearful departure. Bridget O'Connor slipped on a dressing gown and followed the distraught woman outside.

Despite his efforts to brush aside the incident, Victor's party nosedived. No one really felt in the mood for any serious sex after the confrontation between Mary and her son-in-law. Besides, most of the men had already climaxed a number of times and were happy to stand around sipping their drinks, occasionally groping the remaining three females.

With a stifled curse of irritation, Victor left the big lounge and climbed upstairs to where he imagined that Mary had gone. To his surprise, he saw the door to the roof garden open. Sighing heavily, he mounted the steep stairs, wondering what he would have to say to her in order to retrieve the situation. Somehow he didn't think it would be all that simple...

Chapter 7

At the top of the stairs, Victor paused and called out Mary's name. There was no response, but he could hear someone moving around the rooftop garden, the scrape of a chair on the wooden deck. He climbed further until he exited into the bright sunshine. Shielding his eyes, he saw a female form against the light. But it wasn't Mary.

"Why hello, if it isn't Mrs. O'Connor... Bridget. I didn't know you were up here."

"Oh, I came to see if I could help Mary. But I got sidetracked by the truly magnificent view you get from up here."

The attractive blonde turned and, hand on the wooden rail that ran around the perimeter of the flat rooftop garden, she looked out once more as if to appreciate the townscape.

Victor joined her and placed a proprietary arm around her shoulder. If he noticed Bridget's very slight flinch of disgust, he showed no signs of having done so.

"Hey, Bridget, hope you enjoyed the party. Did you get lucky? Let's see..." and so saying, he peremptorily lifted up her silk dressing gown from behind and briefly felt between her legs.

"Uh-oh! Dry as a bone! We'll have to see what we can do about that... why don't you suck my dick and get it nice and hard? Then I'll give you the fuck of your life, doggie-style, while you enjoy the view..."

"Okay, Victor, but let's go over here... it's getting hot up here and there's some shade in this corner."

She let the front of her dressing gown fall open to reveal her stunning figure: superb, firm breasts, flat tummy and a neat, triangular blonde fleece. Bridget gently manoeuvred the stationery tycoon against the wooden railings. When they were in position, she squatted down so that her head was just level with Victor's genitals. She saw that his cock was already stiffening in obscene little jerks and by the time that she had forced herself to take him in her mouth he was almost hard. She felt his hands go around her head and his fingers became entwined in her thick, golden hair. She looked up at him and thought, Victor, you're really a very good-looking guy. With a nice cock. Pity you're such a sick bastard. Such a pity... and such a waste...

"Hey, baby, whatcha doin'? Don't get up now! I'm not finished yet..."

But Bridget now stood directly in front of him. He hadn't realised until then that she was tall for a woman... and that body was very well toned.

"Oh, but I think you are Victor. I think you're quite finished, *baby*!"

And with that she gave him a hard little push, just enough for him to lose his balance and fall back heavily against the wooden railings. Victor looked annoyed and struggled to regain his equilibrium. But the wood gave an ominous cracking sound and instead, he seemed to fall further back still, until the railing snapped entirely.

There was an almost comic moment when Victor's expression changed from irritation to surprise, from surprise to panic and finally from panic to sheer terror as he realised that he was about to plunge into the parking lot over a hundred feet below. Bridget noted that, as he fell, he let out more of a squawk than a scream. No one would hear him until he hit the tarmac, she thought, and that noise would most likely be drowned by the sound of traffic. And now she needed to establish her alibi. Where the hell was Mary?

"I'm here."

Bridget realised that she had spoken the last thought out loud when the nude Chinese woman stepped out of the shadows and came to stand beside her. Together they looked at Victor Jordan's body far below and the dark halo of blood around his head that slowly grew larger.

"What a terrible accident."

Bridget nodded and went to Mary's open arms. The two women hugged, each feeling and enjoying the comforting warmth of the other's flesh. Mary raised her head slightly to whisper in Bridget's ear.

"I saw you push him. It was no accident, was it?"

Bridget shook her head and and gave a grim little smile.

"It's okay. I'll say that I saw him step back, lose his balance and fall heavily against the railings. Honey, I would have done it if I'd had your guts – in fact I wish I'd had the chance. But how did you know that the railings would

give at that particular point if you've never been up here before?

"I'll keep that as my secret, if that's all right with you, Mary."

"Of course it is, honey. We better go and break the sad news."

The two women composed themselves to look suitably stricken and then quickly went down to tell the others.

Epilogue

Two years had passed. After Victor's tragic and untimely death (and which death is ever timely?) Mary Douglas continued to live in Victor Jordan's triplex penthouse, although she had had it completely redecorated. For some reason, she was particularly fond of the roof garden, although the wooden railings had now been replaced by metal ones, since they had been found to be rotten in several places. Her daughter had spent six weeks in therapy to emerge an entirely different, confident young woman. Within months she had met and wedded a local teacher and they had soon settled down to a blissful married life. There was already talk of having children.

And now Jessica Jordan was rich. Wisely, she had sold Victor's family business, but had kept the real estate which would only increase in value over the years as Fairview grew in size. A case in point was the apartment building in which her mother now lived. The rent on the apartments went to give her mother a more than generous living allowance, but of course there was plenty more money available should

Mary ever need it. But Mary's happiness wasn't just dependent on this material security that she had craved so long: her emotional life had taken a turn for the better, too.

Soon after 'the accident', as they all referred to it, Mary had invited Bridget O'Connor to move in with her child and become her paid housekeeper, an offer that was quickly accepted by the young divorcee. That the two women shared a bedroom – indeed a bed – was not commented upon, for the simple reason that nobody in Fairview knew of their sleeping arrangements.

The erotic storm that had rocked their lives had lasted no more than a couple of months. Mary and Jessie would talk about those events but rarely, and then only with much circumspection: there were too many painful memories. Mary never told Jess the true circumstances of Victor's violent end. Besides, everything had worked out for the best, really. But sometimes mother and daughter would lie awake at night, next to their respective partners, and think back to the time when they had been forced to surrender their bodies to each other and consequently experience a love that was, in its own way, quite unique.

The End

HAVANA HARLOT

Pierre Motteux

PAST VENUS HISTORICAL
Period erotica by modern authors

Millionaire businessman Charles (Charlie) Hiram Longworthy takes his family on a visit to Havana in 1910, expecting to enjoy a pleasant holiday and do a little business. When an unscrupulous Cuban gang kidnaps his pretty 17-year-old daughter Helen, his whole world is turned upside-down.

In an attempt to defy the kidnappers Charlie unintentionally places his whole family in jeopardy when they, too, are kidnapped. He, his beautiful, elegant wife, his handsome young son and Helen, all become the sexual playthings of the gang. Worse still, they are forced to perform acts of unspeakable depravity with one another. Escape is the only option.

SISTER'S DIRTY SECRET

Meg Oliphant

PAST VENUS PRESS
20th century erotic pulp classics

When Kathy Walters finds herself a grass widow, her ne'er-do-well younger brother Ned steps in to fill the vacuum in her life. In a degrading spiral of sexual lust, he drags her down to his own level of freewheeling, hedonistic existence. Kathy is appalled by the incestuous tryst she has succumbed to with her own brother, especially as she knows that her husband Don is soon returning from Vietnam.

But Don is no angel either. His experiences with the bar girls of Saigon have changed him for life, not least his encounter with two of Mama Nu's best girls, Xuan and Diu who provide him with sex his wife cannot. Or so he thinks. The scene is set for an explosive collision of carnality and guilt, incest and nymphomania.

£7.50

with sexually explicit illustrations

ORGY GIRL

Robert Bourne

PAST VENUS PRESS
20th century erotic pulp classics

Orgy Girl. Not everyone's desired soubriquet perhaps, but beautiful and statuesque New Yorker Karen Shaw wants the title so badly that she's prepared to fight tooth and nail to get it. From the Hamptons to Manhattan's fashionable upper eastside, this orgiastic young Amazon is in hot demand.

Orgies are what she is looking for and group sex is what she gets. In a spectacular, jet-setting round of outrageous sex parties and hedonistic fun with threesomes, foursomes and moresomes, Karen moves from New York to the Virgin Islands and from there to Paris. Containing lesbian sex, anal sex, incest, sado-masochism, urination and, oh yes, lots of group sex.

£7.50

with sexually explicit illustrations

SATAN'S VIRGIN TWINS

John Langhorne

PAST VENUS PRESS
20th century erotic pulp classics

The twins are nearing their 21st birthday. Daphne is marrying banker Tony Jerrolde and has asked her sister Pam to come to the engagement party. But neither twin realises that they are being drawn into a spider's web of satanic intrigue and demonic lust, where their very lives are at stake.

This is the gripping tale of five young people who must take part in obscene blasphemies and horrific sexual rites in order to thwart Satan's grand plan to reclaim his earthly dominion. Twins and friends must all risk their bodies, their sanity and their very souls in order for their daring ploy to stand a chance. A Past Venus Fantasy masterpiece!